CYNDI
RAYE
Stealing
Her Heart
THE BELLES OF WYOMING SERIES

The Belles of Wyoming series presents

Stealing Her Heart

by
Cyndi Raye

---

[1]. http://www.CyndiRaye.com

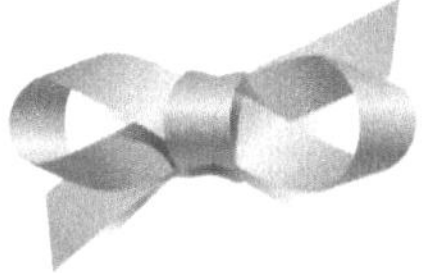

The Creation of Belle, Wyoming

The story behind the missing bells of Belle, Wyoming.
On a wagon train to Oregon in the 1840's, Clara Brown's husband died of Cholera, leaving her on her own. The wagon train did not allow single women to travel alone, so she is ordered to leave.
She was rescued by a trapper and they fell deeply in love, creating their own town not far from Ft. Bridger. They named the town Belle for the jingle bells that were tied on her oxen when they first met. Now, years later, each Christmas the tradition continues as the town places the bells on an ox or horse, gifting rides to remember the legacy of the founders. The bells were safely put away and only brought out each year for this purpose.
Except, this year, the bells have gone missing.
Are they ever found?
This was how the town of Belle began. We've added more stories and authors for each round and hope you enjoy them all

Chapter 1

"**M**artha!"

She hurried inside, carrying a pile of dry cloth bandages she took off the wash line. "What is it, Mercy?"

The doctor's office was closed for lunch, but there was a man on the table with his hand bleeding all over his clothes.

Martha didn't hesitate when she saw him, but took a few of the cloths and helped Mercy stop the bleeding.

"It looks like you may need a stitch or two," Mercy told him. "Doctor Frank will be right back. He went to see an elderly patient over his lunch hour. He checks on him and takes him a special cream for his joints."

Martha shook her head. "I thought he made it clear to old man Parson that he had to walk here for the ointment so he gets some exercise?"

"He did. But, Parson's feet hurt him today. He sent one of the neighborhood kids to ask someone to stop by. You know Frank will not allow anyone else to check in on the old man. They are like father and son."

It was true. Martha had been working part-time at the doctor's office for a few months now, ever since she moved into Mercy's old house. Mercy and Frank fell in love with each other. They had been neighbors since childhood. Old man Parson became part of that family. Before Mercy and Frank, he'd been an old, lonely and bitter man. Now he was loved by most people. As long as they understood his grumpy demeanor.

"I guess it wouldn't be too much to ask if the bleeding has stopped?"

Martha looked up at the man sitting patiently while the two of them discussed Parson. When she looked into his bright blue eyes, Martha felt almost shy. He was quite a handsome man, well-groomed and tall and muscular, although she shouldn't be looking at that.

Mercy wrapped another cloth around the one that was soaking through. "I'm so sorry, sir. We have an elderly patient that we care about. As a newcomer to town, you'll find out how Belle takes care of their own. How do you feel? Are you dizzy at all?"

He shook his head. "No. Just mad at myself for trying to use a saw when I was in a hurry."

Martha watched the man. He said he wasn't hurting, but there were small lines on his forehead that told a different story.

Frank came through the front door just in time. The bell jingled as he closed it. He shrugged off his jacket and replaced it with a white, long sleeved jacket. Throwing a stethoscope around his neck, he ran a hand through his hair and turned to his new patient. "Why, hello. I'm sorry I was not here to greet you. What do we have here?"

The man grunted. "I sliced my hand."

"Indeed." Frank walked over to the basin and poured water on his hands. He was very sanitary when it came to his patients. After he dried his hands, he began to unravel the blood soaked towels. "Let me take a look. Your name, sir?"

"It's Duke. Duke Callahan."

Martha laid a hand on the patient's shoulder when he grimaced as Frank worked on his hand. "It will be okay. Doctor Frank is an excellent physician," she told him softly.

He looked up at her with those disturbing blue eyes and it gave Martha quite a shock. He seemed to look right through to her very soul. She had been done with men since her husband had walked out on her and her ten-year old son Carson awhile back. Now, a flutter of hope stirred inside of her.

She took a step back, fearful of where these thoughts were taking her and especially this man who seemed to stare right through her. There was no way he was interested in someone like her.

"No, no, Martha. Do continue to hold his arm steady. I've got his wrist, but the doctor will need to stitch it up."

Martha had no choice but to get closer. She closed her eyes briefly, just long enough to pull herself together. This was her job. At least for now.

While the doctor stitched the hand, he tried to make small talk with his new patient. "Where are you staying, Mr. Callahan?"

"You can call me Duke. I bought that old mansion down the street. The one Thomas Rider owned. Got it at a bargain price."

Doctor Frank shook his head. "You've got more than a cut hand to worry about with that property. The place is a shambles. It needs a lot of work and it doesn't look like you will be getting too much done in the next few weeks."

Duke seemed upset about the doc's words. "I can't be held back. My family is going to be here in two months time. I've promised them a new home and I'm going to keep my word."

His family? That meant he was probably already married. But, when Martha looked at his hand, she didn't see a ring on his finger. Yet, she knew there were many married men who never wore a ring. She knew her former husband never did.

"Well, son, it doesn't look good for the next week. You can't be using a saw or the stitches will come out. Is there inside work you can do?"

Duke nodded. "What I need is a housekeeper. Someone to go through the tons of stuff that is already inside the house. The man who lived there left piles of stuff. Old photographs, pictures of members of his family I'd guess and papers that need taken out and burned."

"You may have to hire yourself outside workers as well for the time being. There are also plenty of young men and some older fellows that are looking for work. Don't be afraid to utilize them. If you put up a notice at the mercantile, you may get a ton of help. They may work for some of the stuff left over in the house if you plan on bringing new furniture in."

Martha didn't want to interrupt their conversation but an idea crossed her mind. Now, if she could forget he was such a handsome fellow and think of her son she'd be alright. "I can use an extra job."

Frank and Mercy both looked up from what they were doing? Mercy spoke up. "Oh, Martha! I didn't know you needed more work. I'm sorry, we just don't have enough business to give you any more hours."

She didn't want to upset them. "Oh, please, Mercy. What you and Doc Frank have done for me is much more than I ever imagined. It's just Carson would like to be a doctor some day."

"That's great news," the doctor mentioned. His smile ran from ear to ear. "I can put in a good word for him when the time comes. Maybe show him some things when he gets a little older."

Martha smiled. The doctor meant well. But, money was what she needed in order to give him a better life. If this man was looking for a housekeeper she was great at organizing and cleaning things. "If he is going to go to medical school, then I need to start saving money now. If I work extra jobs, I may be able to send him someday."

Duke Callahan watched her intently. "I do need a housekeeper. If you'd like the job, you can work the hours around your position here. It will be approximately two months until my family arrives. I'd pay you well. Plus, if you'd like to stay on after they arrive, we can also discuss it down the road."

Martha gave him a smile. "I think this is the easiest interview for a position I've ever received. Thank you, Mr. Callahan."

He nodded. "It's Duke."

Mercy was watching the exchange between the two of them. When Martha looked over, she saw the devilment in her friend and co-worker's eyes. A silent warning before she turned away had Mercy giggle out loud.

This was going to be an interesting job. Besides there was another reason she wanted the job as housekeeper and it had nothing to do with the handsome Duke or the money.

It had to do with proof of who she was.

No one in this town knew anything about her that she didn't want them to know.

And as far as she was concerned, she'd never tell a soul. But, she had to get inside that house to get rid of the evidence. This was the perfect chance to finally do so.

Before Duke Callahan or anyone else in town found out.

Chapter 2

Duke struggled to stand. He felt a bit wobbly after getting seven stitches in his hand. The way the doc had his hand wrapped up so well he wouldn't be able to move it for a week. "Thank you, Doc. I'll be sure to do as instructed."

Doctor Frank gave him a pat on the shoulder. "In Belle, I like to check up on my patients. I'll stop by the mansion tomorrow sometime to see how you are feeling. If you feel faint or start to run a fever, get back here, no matter what time of day."

"I don't want to disturb you if you are closed, Doc."

"No need to worry. I have an open door policy and as long as no one takes advantage, it works out well. Most people will try to wait until office hours to see me. Everyone knows my rule and if it is an emergency, I will expect a knock no matter when."

"Yes, sir." For a young doctor, he was quite forceful. Duke paid up and left, letting Miss Winslow know he'd expect her in the morning to get started. She opened and closed her eyes and lowered her head, nodding.

As Duke walked down the street towards the mansion, he wondered about her. She was a beautiful woman, fire red hair and skin that glowed. He wondered if she realized how lovely she was.

"Mr. Callahan! Wait up!"

Miss Winslow was hurrying towards him. In her hand she held a small bottle. "You forgot your tincture."

He stopped abruptly and swung around. She had almost been on top of him and he reached out his good hand to stop her from running full force into him. She breathed heavily, holding one hand over her heart. "I'm so sorry, but I wanted to get this to you. Doctor Frank forgot to give you some fever-few for your pain."

He stared at the dark bottle. "What do I do with it? I never heard of fever-few."

When she smiled at him, her face transformed. Those green eyes locked onto his own blue ones and she was confident when she spoke. It was nice to see her coming out of her shell.

Except he wondered why she was hiding in one in the first place? Had someone tried to hurt her?

"This is derived from leaves. It is dried and made into a tincture. All you need to do is add about two to three drops in water, or any liquid if you want some relief. I'm sure later this evening your hand may start to thump."

When she handed over the bottle, their fingers touched. She shot back as if her fingers were on fire.

Interesting.

Was she aware of how much he wanted to gaze into her eyes and get to know her? He had to be honest. He wanted to kiss her.

She was that intriguing.

He held back since he was going to hire her to clean his house.

"I have to get back to work, but I'll see you first thing in the morning. I have a ten year old son who may have to come along some days. Right now he is in school, but there may be a day or two school is not in session. Is that acceptable?"

Duke shrugged. "I don't see why not. Maybe he'd like to contribute and save up for his college fund. Will you allow me to ask him?"

Martha looked surprised. No one ever thought about her son working to earn his own money. "If you'd like to. I'm sure he'd be excited to help work."

"Very good then. I'll see you tomorrow." He watched as she hurried off down the street. The next few weeks were indeed going to be interesting. At least he had some help for the inside of the house.

A sigh escaped him as he made his way through the old iron gate and down the yard towards the porch. It looked like someone had tried to start a garden at one time, but weeds had overgrown most of the effort. Weeds grew where fresh vegetables probably should be planted.

An old man walked slowly past the house. He slowed his steps when he realized Duke was on the porch. He stared hard.

"Hello, sir," Duke offered, waving his good hand.

"What did you do?" the old man asked.

"Cut my hand on a saw. It took a few stitches to close it up."

His ageing body came to a stand still as he held onto a wooden cane to keep him steady. "That was a dumb move. Doc says I need to walk at least to your house and back several times a day. Just so you don't think I care about what goes on here, I am under doctor's orders."

Duke chuckled. The man was outspoken. "I thank you for letting me know. I'm sure I'd notice if someone were snooping around."

Old man Parson cackled. "You don't have to worry none about me. I'm the last person who would snoop around. I'll just come out and ask you if I want to know anything. What do you want that big old house for, a lone man like you?"

"I won't be alone for long. My mother and sister will be joining me. I promised them a new start."

"Well, what's wrong with the life they got?"

He was persistent, but Duke didn't mind. The old man was harmless. "Considering my step-father was trying to weasel my mother's horse farm from her, I'd say she is ready to move on and go somewhere quiet. Belle seems to be that place."

"Horse farm?"

Was that all he heard? Duke nodded. "My father owned a horse farm in Kentucky. Raised some fine horses. When she remarried, the scoundrel sold a bunch of fine horseflesh and almost sold the place out from under the family. Luckily, our neighbors found out and revealed the truth to my mother. She had him thrown in jail."

"How is she coming out here if she owns a farm?"

"She sold the farm to our neighbors. At least they'll give it the respect it deserves and a good price to my mother. She's getting older and wants to take life easy. I promised her by the time she got here, I'd have a place for her to retire."

Old man Parson began to laugh. He even slapped his knee then winced.

"What's so funny?"

"You want to bring her there?" He pointed to Duke's new house.

"I plan to fix it up some."

"That's the funniest thing I ever heard. You have a lot of work to do. It will take a bunch of Sundays to get that wreck of a house fixed up."

He wanted to tell the old man to mind his business, but instead he let out a deep breath. "Yeah, I didn't know it was this bad. I've got a housekeeper starting tomorrow who is going to help me."

"Who is that?"

His questions never ended. "Martha Winslow. She works for the doc part time. Said she needed more money to put her kid through medical school."

The old man nodded. "I heard the boy wants to be a doctor." He raised his cane in the air almost as if pointing to Duke. "You be careful with those two. They've been through a lot of hard times."

That was why she hung her head so. He wanted to ask what kind of hard times, but before he had a chance, the old man told him. "Her divorce is finally through. Glad we have a good lawyer here in Belle so she could get rid of that no-gooder. If he ever steps foot in Belle, I'll be the first one to shoot him in the arse with my pistol."

Was Parson dangerous or just an old man forgetting he was no longer capable of hurting someone? Duke chose the latter, knowing the old man was probably lonely. His mother sometimes went on and on when she wanted attention. "It sounds like she was treated poorly."

Parson nodded and shook his finger at Duke. "Not only that, the boy was cut by his own father with a large, sharp knife. Had stitches worse than yours. His arm was in bad shape for a long time. Like I said, he's not welcome in this town and the sheriff will make sure of it. No one messes with the people of Belle."

Duke took it as a warning from a concerned citizen and he didn't blame the old man. It sounded like a horrible thing to happen to a child. He knew one thing, he was going to work at putting a smile on Martha's face. But, he was going to be the perfect employer and respect her above all else. He wanted to show her not every man was like her husband.

Even if he did want to hold her and kiss her sweet mouth.

Chapter 3

Martha dropped Carson off at school and headed quickly towards the mansion. She had placed her bright red hair in a tight bun under a covering this morning. Martha was dying to let it flow free like some of the newer styles, but she was afraid to. All her life people mentioned how bright her hair was so she always tried to downplay it.

Growing up with such vivid red hair was troublesome. She did love the color but was always hesitant to leave it uncovered when she was out and about. People always stared as if she were a sore spot in the middle of a beautiful world.

When she married her husband, he had forced her to hide her hair under bonnets and coverings even inside when they got company, telling her it was embarrassing that people stared. She had gotten used to it over the years, wrapping a cloth around her head so he didn't get upset. Now that he was a part of her history, she wondered if it really mattered now since times were changing.

The man who got hurt, Duke Callahan, didn't seem bothered by her bright red hair. She didn't cover it inside the doctor's office, only when going outside. Thinking about yesterday, he seemed intrigued instead of repulsed when he looked into her eyes.

She turned off of Main Street and onto Pine Tree Lane where the mansion he bought sat halfway down the street. Passing the house she rented from Mercy, she sighed. The front porch was filled with plants and potted flowers that Mercy had left behind when she moved in next door with Frank. She loved sitting outside in the evening enjoying her new life, surrounded by nature's beauty.

Since Frank opened his doctor's office in his family home, Mercy had worried the patients who waited on the porch might have a reaction to some of the pretty plants. A few of their patients had allergies according to Doctor Frank. Martha was glad to have the plants and flowers Mercy left behind. Watering them in the late evening was quite relaxing, something she hadn't felt for a long, long time.

She had to admit, these past few months were happy days for her and Carson. Since her husband left, the relief she felt knowing he wasn't going to come home all liquored up and try to hurt one of them helped her sleep all night long instead of in one-hour intervals. It had been hard to function with little sleep during that period of her life. He was long gone and she didn't have to worry about him any longer. Besides, he wouldn't know where to find them since they no longer lived in the same house.

The paperwork for the divorce was finalized. Even if he tried to come back here, she'd call for Sheriff Knight and he promised to have him arrested for what he did to Carson.

Everyone loved Carson. He was the sweetest ten year old ever. He made friends where ever he went and he loved to fish. Since he didn't have a father to do things with him, many times the men in Belle would ask him to go along fishing. There was always fresh fish to cook for supper, for which Martha was thankful for. She didn't have to worry about putting food on the table. One less thing to worry about.

She was able to make ends meet but there was no extra money to put Carson through medical school someday. Time was flying by and she knew that this job as a housekeeper would give her the extra money to stash away for the said purpose of Carson's education. Even if she had to work with a handsome man like Duke Callahan, she'd do her job diligently so he was able to bring his family here to Belle.

She walked by the doctor's office and waved when one of the patients sitting on the bench outside recognized her. Since she was on the other side of the street, she kept walking, not stopping to chat since she didn't want to be late.

There was another reason she took the housekeeping job. When Thomas Rider, the man who previously owned the mansion, had been taken to the insane asylum, all of his belongings were left behind. No one came to claim them and Martha knew why. He didn't have any relatives alive.

At least that anyone knew about.

Except for her and she was not about to associate herself with a crazy man who tried to hurt Mercy. He had been obsessed with the doctor's wife to the point he kidnapped her and tried to harm her. Thank God he got caught.

No one in this town knew Thomas Rider was her uncle. Her mother had warned her about the crazy man he was and to stay away from him. The family had disowned him after Thomas's mother had died. When Martha came back home, she never let anyone know he was her uncle since he never saw her after she grew up and got married. It was why they were able to live in the same town together. But she knew her Aunt Regina, Thomas's mother, had labeled all her photos with the names of their relatives. If anyone looked at the photos and saw her name, she'd be doomed.

There was a time when Thomas had behaved like a normal person. She remembered how he'd play outside and swim in the creek with them during family get togethers. For some reason no one ever mentioned why, her family had moved away from Belle when she was seven, but she had remembered the place and came back when she married.

Martha had been glad to come back home, but terrified at first that Thomas would recognize her. Her mother had warned her when she was young to never be alone with him. She had said he was a strange and evil man and to stay away from him. Martha had listened to her mother and she never saw him again until she was grown. Then when she walked past him one day on Main Street, he looked right at her and she knew he had no idea who she was. After that, she didn't worry if they ran into each other.

After she had Carson, she avoided Thomas Rider at all costs, staying away from Pine Tree Lane. Her mother's warnings that he was not right in the head had bothered her more now that she had a child of her own. Plus, once her son got older, she didn't think it would be right to introduce the crazy man as a relative.

It was better for Carson that he never found out who Thomas Rider was. People were cruel and didn't understand. She didn't need her boy being made fun of if they found out he was related to the strange man who lived in the mansion. Carson's troubles with his father were hard enough. At least she was able to protect him from being teased.

She knew there were family photos in that house and she was going to go through every single room until she found them and could destroy any evidence that she was related to the man. In a way, Martha felt bad for even thinking this way. She wasn't ashamed of her family, but she didn't want the stigma of having a crazy person in the family to affect her son. She'd do anything to protect her son at this point.

She had worried often that if Carson found out, or anyone in town knew, they'd think Carson may be crazy as well. She didn't want him growing up having to pay for another person's dysfunction. No, she'd protect her son at all costs.

As long as the house had stayed empty she hadn't worried about anyone finding those photos. But after he almost hurt Mercy, the town wanted to remove any reminders that Thomas Rider had lived here. They put up notices about the property in Belle and in newspapers in cities as far east as New York City and Philadelphia. After forty-five days the house was put up for sale by the city of Belle. As is. The family photos were still there. They needed to be found and removed.

Now that she was hired as a housekeeper, it would be easy to get rid of them. While Mr. Callahan was busy she'd find them and destroy them. Even bury them in the back yard if she had to, but she wasn't leaving that house until they were all found.

Martha would not leave a trace behind for her son to suffer by. Not if her life depended on it.

Before Martha realized she had walked so far, she was at the property. The gate squeaked when she went through. The walkway was crowded with weeds, but she found her way to the front porch and lifted her hand to knock. A voice behind her made her jump and screech! She swung around to find Duke Callahan standing there, a huge smile on his face.

"You scared the daylights out of me!" Her hand flew to her heart. It pumped so fast she sucked in a deep breath to help slow it down.

He actually bowed and apologized. "I'm sorry. I did not mean to startle you. I was trying to clear the yard somewhat but it is quite difficult to do so one-handed. I heard someone out front here and came around the side of the house."

She actually laughed, her voice echoing in the fresh morning air. "I'm sorry then to have made such a ruckus. I'm here to get started."

He nodded. "Did you get your son off to school?"

It was nice that he asked about Carson. "Yes, he loves school. Plus, he has some friends there as well. He gets so excited each morning. Most kids don't like school, but he wants to learn."

Duke came up the steps, standing in front of her on the porch. "Well, then, he'll be appreciative that you are starting a fund for his medical school education. I believe he'll make a fine doctor if he likes learning already."

Martha was surprised he was so interested in her son. He didn't seem the type who cared one way or another. She wondered what kind of work he did. She didn't like to be nosey, but she wasn't afraid to ask. Working for the doctor, she had watched how Mercy engaged the patients to talk. It had been quite easy once she paid attention. A few questions was all it took some days to get people talking, especially when it was about themselves.

"Mr. Callahan, where do you hail from, if you don't mind me asking?"

"Not at all. I may have told you yesterday that my parents had a horse farm in Kentucky. I grew up there, but spent the last few years in New York City."

"I see." She had forgotten he mentioned it yesterday at the doc's office. "What kind of work do you do?"

He hesitated for a moment and stared at her.

Was he trying to hide what he did for a living?

She stared at him with uplifted brows. Why was he hesitating and what kind of man was ashamed of his work? Besides, she should know if she was going to be working for him.

Was he hiding something, too? Because in Belle it was hard to hide anything. Sooner or later someone would find out. That was why she had to get rid of the evidence inside this home.

She had to do it quickly before her son was damaged for life. When her husband left town she vowed no one would ever hurt him again. She meant every single word she had promised him.

Even if it meant deceiving this dashingly handsome man.

"I worked in banking."

"A bank teller?"

"You could say that." He seemed aloof when it came to his job. He *was* hiding something. She found it interesting. One thing Martha had noticed even before working for Belle's doctor was that not everyone was quite what they seemed. Just went to show there were many skeletons in people's closets and no one was perfect.

"Well, then, you know I need to make some money here today to put my son through medical school. Shall we get started?"

He seemed to come out of his trance. He had been staring at a spot on her hair. He blinked several times and moved to the front door. "Yes, of course."

"I'll make sure to do a wonderful job so your wife and children can move in without any issues at hand."

Duke Callahan turned to her, his eyes wide and his mouth opened. Then he snapped it shut and turned away.

Martha wasn't quite sure what that was all about, but she followed him inside.

Chapter 4

Duke froze. He didn't want anyone in this town to know the extent of his fortune. In the city he had been well-known as the owner of the Brooklyn Bank of International Commodities. He had sold his company to make the move here, rendering him a millionaire. Between his mother selling her horse farm and the sale of his bank, they'd never have to worry again.

People had always been polite and kind to him because of his wealth. Most tried to swindle money. Even the ladies were the same, trying to latch onto a man with money. At first he liked the city life and all it had to offer. Then it got tiresome, not knowing who truly cared. He had been brought up as a southern gentleman and he tried to be kind to others, but the greed in their faces and eyes were too much.

When his mother had written him about the con-man she had married and how he had tried to swindle her, Duke made a decision and vow to make sure they were always taken care of. The horse farm had been his father's dream. His mother had enough to worry about taking care of his sister. And for his sister's sake, and by the urging of her physician, they decided as a family the mountain air would be better for her.

As he answered Martha's questions, he made a quick and probably ludicrous decision not to be directly honest with her. It wasn't that he wanted to keep anything from her. She seemed honest and sincere. But the less she knew about him, the better. He wanted to start over in a new place where people didn't judge him because he was wealthy. When she mentioned a wife and children, he didn't say anything, just let her believe that's who was coming.

Was it awful to deceive her like this?

He was torn between blurting out the truth, that there was no wife or children and yet he wanted to get to know her before he made that admission. After all, he didn't say either way who was coming to Belle, and the less anyone knew the better. He did tell old man Parson, but hopefully the old coot wouldn't remember.

"This room will need to be done as soon as the kitchen gets finished."

The parlor was a mess. There was some furniture in the room and a large desk against one wall. Clothes were strewn from one end of the room to the other as if the prior owner used the parlor as his dressing room.

The look in her eyes was quite interesting. She was appalled at the extent of cleaning that was needed and yet when she turned and looked at him he also saw a determination in her eyes that lifted his spirits. She wasn't going to back down from the challenge. "If you show me where the supplies are, I'll get started right away."

He made his way to the kitchen where he had tried to wash up some of the dishes that were still setting out. "I didn't have much luck getting anything accomplished since the house is such a mess," he told her, hoping she'd realize this wasn't his doing. "I'm afraid the prior owner was not neat and orderly at all."

"He was a disgusting mess."

"I'm sorry."

She gave him an incredulous look. "Why would you be sorry? You are not responsible for what someone else does."

He shrugged. "No, I am not. But, looking around I'm sure this is going to be quite a job for you. I'll tell you what, if you can finish this room and the kitchen by the end of the month, I will pay you double of what I had intended."

Her eyes got huge! "Double? Are you able to do so?"

He hesitated at first. Then, walked over to the desk where some of his own things were sitting. Alfred Dunhill had opened a luxury line of men's messenger bags and gifted him with one. It was one of the best gifts he ever received. He opened the lock and felt around in the one compartment for a brown envelope that held some cash. As a former banker, he realized the value of having cash to bargain with and make purchases that may take longer than with a line of credit. He knew how banks operated sometimes.

He took some bills and handed them to Martha. "This is your first month's wages. If you can finish the two rooms within that time, I'll double this at the end of the month."

Martha hesitated before accepting the money. Her eyes were wary but she held out her hand. Counting the bills, she froze. Her eyes went from the thick envelope to stare at him. He wasn't sure what her reaction was going to be until she spoke.

"This is too much money to clean a house." She handed the money back to him but he took a step back.

"I need you to work hard. I may need you helping to do other things to accommodate my family. We have to go through all the prior owner's belongings. Some may be sent to the church if it is salvageable."

"No one in this town wants the prior owner's things. They should all be burned."

"You have your work cut out for you, then. Please, I insist you accept this money and the challenge to get it done by the end of the month. I put away plenty of cash for this purpose. It is important I have a good, clean place for my family to come to."

Martha smirked.

He stared. "Why the smirk?"

She lifted her chin a bit. "I can get this done in two weeks. Since you have so much cash floating around, how about tripling it if I can get it done in half the time?"

She was crafty! Martha had noticed his thick envelope with all his cash. He grinned. "You got yourself a deal."

A blush slowly covered her cheeks. Duke thought she was even prettier now that she showed some personality.

"I am not usually so blunt. Please, accept my apology."

He liked this forceful side of Martha. "You aren't going back on your challenge are you? Are you worried now that it can't be done? Did you speak too soon?"

She placed a hand on her hip. "Of course not. Why, after lugging all this stuff to the back yard to burn, I can clean the walls and floors in a day's time." Her mouth snapped shut.

"I do believe you've mapped out a strategy already, Miss Winslow." He had no intention of letting her do it all herself. He'd carry what he could outside, even if he had to use one hand to get it done.

She gave the kitchen a once over. "Before anything gets taken outside to burn, I need to make a decent area for you to make your meals. I'll start in here." When Martha turned away, Duke watched her for a few moments before going back outside. He wanted her to feel comfortable in the big mansion without him being in her way. She seemed to know what she was doing.

She also went right to a hook on the back door in the kitchen where an apron hung. She pulled it down, shook the dust off and tied it around her waist. "Now, if you will excuse me, I have work to do," she told him when she realized he was still watching her.

Growing up with a stern mother and sister in the house he knew that was his order to disappear. Which he didn't mind one bit. "I have a few errands to run. I'll be back within a few hours."

Duke slipped out of the house, determined to stay out of her way for now. They'd have plenty of time to work together in the days ahead. Would he be able to work side by side with Martha? She was proving to be quite adorable when she got a fire under her feet.

Thoughts of her challenging him kept him entertained as he made his way down Tall Pine past the doctor's office. Mercy was on the porch helping an elderly man inside. It looked like the same man who stopped him and who warned him about treating Martha and her son kindly. "Hello, Mr. Callahan. Have you met your neighbor, Mr. Parson yet?"

"Yep, sure did."

Parson grumbled something and Mercy gave him a wide smile. She looked up and shook her head and waved. "Mr. Callahan, can you tell Martha that Carson will be going fishing with the Martins today after school, please? He's going to be staying for supper and they will bring him home around six. Mrs. Martin was here for her check up and wanted me to remind Martha. Mrs. Martin is having a baby in a few months. Thank you and have a good day."

He waved back. "I will let her know." That meant she'd be able to work later. Not that he wanted her to work too hard, but it meant she'd be willing to stay and maybe have supper with him if she didn't have to pick up her son.

He'd have to see what the small café in town had in the way of a good meal. Duke strolled down the street, a pleasant smile on his face. He waved to some of the other residents who raised a hand at him, his step lighter than it had been in a long time.

Chapter 5

A FEW HOURS OF HARD work and Martha was pleasantly surprised at how much she got done. She left the kitchen to find a clock. Thinking she saw one in the parlor, she searched the room until her eyes caught a glimpse of the fancy clock sitting on a side table. The case was hand painted in sea foam and light sage-mint green with flowers intricately decorated over it. She gazed at the open encasement to find it would be another half hour until she had to pick up Carson.

That gave her a chance to work more in the kitchen. She had already cleaned up all the dishes randomly lying around. After soaking, scrubbing and drying, each piece had a place on the wood shelf above the table. It was a wonder bugs hadn't invaded the house as filthy as it was left. A sigh escaped her as she realized what she had done had taken most of the afternoon and there was hardly a dent in the kitchen.

She told Duke it would take her only part of the month to get the two rooms done. Martha ran a hand across her brow, pushing back a stray hair that loosened from her secure bun. Feeling thirsty, she went to get a glass of cool water. One thing that was nice about the mansion was an inside pump that brought the water inside. It set alongside the drain board where she set the dishes to air dry earlier.

As she pumped the water, she heard noises coming from the basement where the cistern was housed. The large holding tank was filled with rainwater and as the water flowed through the pump, it made noises that startled Martha at first. Not every home in Belle had the luxury of an inside pump, but someone had thought to put one in here. She was glad. Not having to lug water from outside would be a huge time saver in the long run. She had filled a pitcher full and set it on the counter in case Duke would get thirsty later.

Martha decided to take her glass to the front porch and sit for a few minutes before she went for her son. It had been a tiresome afternoon. She hadn't worked so hard in a long time. Taking care of the house she lived in with Carson was easy. Her landlord, Mercy, had always taken such good care of the place. All she had to do was clean up after herself and her son, which didn't take long at all. Carson was obedient and put his own things away when asked. After all he'd been through, she couldn't ask for a better child.

"You are so fortunate today, Miss Winslow!" A voice called out from the street. She recognized it immediately and stood up, afraid of getting caught sitting on the job.

"I'm sorry, I was having a glass of water," she called back in greeting. Shame filled her cheeks with a pink blend that almost matched her hair. Strands of it had fallen from the covering she wore. Martha tried to push it back in place.

He waved a hand. "Please, sit back down. I've got a surprise!"

Martha watched as he strolled through the gate, a confident look about him. He held a large basket in one hand. When he came onto the porch where she sat at the small outside table, he set the basket in the middle.

"What do you have there?" she asked, curious.

"Supper."

She thought he must be mighty hungry for someone carrying such a large basket. Had Charity, Joseph's widowed sister, made him a basket with an offer to have supper with him, thinking he was available? It was a terrible way to think, but Duke was a handsome man. Plus, any woman in Wyoming could plainly see there was no ring on his finger. She wondered why.

"Miss Winslow?"

Martha shook herself, not realizing her mind had drifted somewhat. Smiling at her boss, she waited for him to speak again.

"As I was walking past the doctor's office, his wife informed me that your son will be going fishing with the Martin family after school and having supper with them. I believe they will bring him home around six."

"Oh!" Martha was going to heat up leftovers anyway this evening, but this made it even nicer. She could save the leftovers for tomorrow and slice some tomatoes from her garden. A chunk of bread and slices of tomatoes would be plenty to sustain her until breakfast.

"So that is why I decided to pick up something from the café and invite you to have supper right here on the porch with me. Is this acceptable to you, Miss Winslow?"

He pulled back the cloth that covered the basket to find fresh fried chicken and a large covered bowl. The aroma hit her nostrils and she called out without realizing it. "Oh, that smells delicious." Perhaps Martha was hungrier than she realized. She stood. "Let me get some plates and I'll set the table. Why don't you take a load off, Mr. Callahan?"

Duke seemed glad to sit down after lugging the basket from the café. That was quite a walk if one was not used to it, she thought to herself. Martha went inside to gather two plates and forks, along with the pitcher of water she had just pumped. Placing everything on a large tray, she added two cloth napkins after dishing through a pile of cloths in the corner of one of the cabinets.

Martha set a plate out for Duke as well as one for herself. She wasn't shy at all about being invited to eat a meal. The food from the café was always so good but she wasn't able to afford going there often. At times, she'd save enough to get her son something to eat on an occasional night out and order a cup of hot tea for herself. It made him happy and he always shared with her even if she said she wasn't hungry.

When Martha bit into a piece of fried chicken, she moaned. "This is so good," she told Duke with her mouth full. She was unapologetic because she hadn't eaten good food like this in a long time. He was sitting across from her watching with those dark eyes. At first, she almost blushed, but the delicious food she held won out. Bite after bite, she gave a small moan of ecstasy until everything was eaten off the bone.

Realizing she probably looked like a starving maniac, a slow smile spread across her cheek. There was no use being embarrassed. She liked to eat. She gave him a grin right before wiping her mouth and fingers with the napkin on her lap. "That was good."

"You've said that several times," he joked, biting into his own chicken. After chewing slowly, he swallowed, making eating a piece of chicken look rather exciting. Martha could not for the life of her take her eyes off of his mouth. She forced herself to look down at her glass of water and willed her fingers to grab a hold of the water glass.

These tinges of excitement zapping through her was new. Not even her husband in his good days had made her feel so naughty. She wanted to dab his mouth with her napkin when a small piece of meat was left on his lip. Then she wanted to give him a big kiss. Martha stood up, almost knocking her plate to the floor.

He set the chicken on his plate, wiping his mouth before pushing his chair back. "Miss Winslow, are you feeling ill? Did I upset you?" He frowned, looking more confused than she'd ever seen him.

Martha sighed, embarrassed now. She laid a hand over her heart. "I am terribly sorry, Mr. Callahan. I, um, -"

He lifted a hand. "Please, I promise not to say or do anything to offend you. I understand sitting here with me is confusing. We are in the open where anyone walking by can see us. Has this worried you?"

She could lie and say that was the reason for the way she behaved. Perhaps it was best to say nothing at all. Sitting back down, she gave him a reassuring smile. "I'm sorry, it was all too much all of a sudden. Shall we finish eating?"

Duke waited for her to begin eating before he sat back down. He picked up another piece of chicken and ate without saying much. Was he giving her room to feel more comfortable? He thought she had behaved that way because she was sitting alone with a married man. The fact was she had almost ran as fast as her legs would take her because being so close to him was disturbing. The feelings her body stirred up confused her. How was she going to be able to work for this man and stay sane? A married man at that.

Chapter 6

DUKE THOUGHT MARTHA was acting quite strange. As he ate his chicken, she had stared at him, her eyes widening with each bite he took. It was quite interesting that she had watched his mouth and her cheeks became flushed. Was he having that kind of effect on her? The thought made him happy knowing she did have an interest in him as well. It was still too early to tell her that his family did not consist of a wife and children, but his mother and sister.

Duke wanted to be sure she'd want him for himself and not because he had a huge bank account. But outright lying about a family he didn't have was making him feel guilty. He tried to reason with himself, but found his excuses to be rather lame.

The way they were behaving when around each other, he saw sparks were already beginning to fly.

Too quick.

Too soon.

Was there a way to remain friends without wanting to kiss her every single time she was near him? He let the air out from his lung. Was there a way to keep it cordial with her? He frowned again, not realizing she was watching him carefully.

"Is there something wrong?" She was holding her glass of water.

"No. I was just thinking of my family and how nice it will be when they arrive."

"I'm sure you're wife and children will love Belle."

Duke made the decision he was tired of lying to her. He was going to tell her there was no wife or children. He was going to do it as they ate the delicious pie the owner of the café had made. He reached in the basket and pulled it out. "Are you ready for dessert?"

"Is that what I think it is?"

"If you think it is a huge lemon meringue pie then you are right."

"Let me get a knife to cut us each a piece." Martha retreated inside while he waited patiently for her return. Duke was determined he was going to explain why he lied to her. It wasn't really a lie, but wanted to get it straight so they could, what? So he could court her?

Maybe courting was too soon. After all, she was just divorced. And what would his mother think of him courting a divorced woman? Actually, his mother didn't have any place to talk. She was also divorced. Good. One tragedy averted.

What he did know was the red-haired woman coming out through the screen door was making his emotions go wild like a mountain lion on a mission to attack its prey.

"Here we go," she said, handing him a large sharp knife.

He took it and sliced them each a piece of pie, setting one on each plate. As they began to dig in, a noise from the street caught their attention. "I guess I'll go home and drink a cup of coffee by myself," the old man's voice was heard louder than usual.

Martha looked at him, her eyes boring right into his. "I think he wants to be invited for pie."

How was he going to tell her about his wife and kids? Or, lack of, with an old nosey neighbor at the table. He sighed. "Come on up, Mr. Parson. There's plenty of pie for you."

His voice giddy, the old man wobbled up to the porch, thanked them and pulled a chair over to the table. "Now this is what I call neighborly. A year ago I'd never of thought I'd be talking to my next door neighbor."

Martha agreed. "It's true. Mr. Parson was kind of a hermit, weren't you?" She gazed at the old man with delight dancing in her eyes. Duke thought it was sweet the way she seemed to care about the old man.

Parson grunted, shoveling pie in his mouth as if he hadn't eaten all day. "I learned who my friends were. Plus, it helped that Doctor Frank fixed me up. Old Doc Roberts was getting too darn old. He'd rather go fishing than fix me up."

Martha patted his arm. "Well, sir, you are all fixed up and feeling much better. We are glad to have you joining the town's activities. You do know the barn raising is coming up soon. I hope you will attend."

Old man Parson nodded. "I suppose I'll work my way over. Going to be some good food there anyway. I can't help raise the barn, but I can teach them young whipper-snappers a thing or two."

"I'm sure they will be happy to listen to your expert advice, Mr. Parson."

The old man shoved the last piece of pie into his mouth. He turned to Duke. "Hopefully, your mother and sister will get here in time for the barn raising."

Martha looked at him. Then, she looked back at the old man. "What do you mean, Mr. Parson?"

He shrugged. "You know they are heading out this way soon. They sold a horse farm in Kentucky and are moving to our wonderful little town. I still don't know how they are going to be able to stand living in the old Thomas Rider mansion."

He watched as the color drained from her face. She gazed at him once with a furious look, then turned back to Parson. "What about his wife and children?"

"Wife and children? He's not married." The old man looked up in bewilderment. "You aren't married, are you Callahan?"

Duke swallowed. This was not the way he had wanted to tell Martha. With a stoic look, he gazed into her flashing eyes. "No, I am not married. Nor do I have any children."

Parson snorted, looking at Martha like she was crazed. "Whatever gave you that idea?"

Martha stood. Her napkin flew through the air to land on the table. It was not a ladylike move at all.

It was probably good the old man was eyeing the leftover pie. "Mind if I take a piece of this along with me?"

Duke was waiting for her to say something. Instead, she turned to the old man. "I hadn't realized it was so late. My son will be coming home any moment, so I must leave. Goodnight, Mr. Parson. Please, be careful." She gave him a hug and turned to Duke. "Thank you for the meal. It was quite delicious. I enjoyed myself immensely up until the last two minutes. I'll be here first thing in the morning. Goodnight, sir."

Callahan stood. He left it at that. She was too angry to follow and he didn't want to make a spectacle in front of the old man.

Except the old man was more observant than he realized. "What did you do now?" he asked as if this whole thing was his doing.

"What did I do? It's more like what did you do?" Duke sat back down, frowning.

Parson snorted again, which was starting to get annoying. "I didn't do anything except repeat what you told me. Why'd you make up a lie that you were married?"

Duke realized how it sounded. He wasn't a man who could deny the truth. "I didn't want her to know that I have money."

Parson actually looked away from the pie he was obsessed with to stare at Duke. "That's the dumbest reason to lie to a woman I've ever heard of!"

"You're telling me! I don't even know why I told her that. Now she'll never trust anything I say again."

Parson nodded, picking up the knife and cutting him another slice. He wasn't waiting for an answer but taking it upon himself to get more pie. He began to shovel it in his mouth.

Duke realized what he was doing. "You supposed to be eating all that in one sitting? It's going to make you sick."

"Humph. What they don't know won't hurt anyone. I like my pie."

"You get sick don't come bothering me."

The old man guffawed. "You have enough problems, son."

Duke supposed he did. He tangled a web he hoped to get out of. Tomorrow he'd sit her down and tell her the truth. Everything except how much money he had. That was truly no one's business.

Chapter 7

Martha was still furious, even after spending the night trying to reason with herself. When she thought back to the exact conversation, she had realized Duke never actually told her who was coming. He had said his family. She was the one who mentioned a wife and children, even though he didn't deny it.

Was she upset because now she had nothing in the way of a barrier to keep him at a distance? He had looked at her several times as if he wanted to kiss her. He had made her feel like she was a beautiful woman and it gave her a feeling like she had never felt before.

The problem with all those feelings was it wasn't real. Knowing he had a wife and children on their way made it easy for Martha to pretend he was untouchable. It made her feel safe the first day she went into his home alone with him.

Now, she'd enter his home knowing he could possibly kiss her at any time. She wasn't ready for a relationship, yet she kept getting drawn to Mr. Callahan.

Martha didn't think she'd ever want another man again, not after her husband and all he'd done to her. All those lonely nights he never came home to find he was with another woman! The drunkenness that occurred when he did come home and the fear it instilled inside of her. Her protectiveness with her child and all the years she had to hide him to keep the boy safe from a drunkard who didn't even remember when he struck his own son or wife. All these emotions came tumbling from her mind all night long.

She dropped Carson off at school and began the long walk towards the mansion. When she turned on Tall Pine Lane, she wondered if Duke would still want her to work for him. Maybe he'd fire her. Then what? She'd never be able to save enough money for Carson to go to medical school. She'd have to convince him she had been too emotional and explain why. At least she wanted to be honest. If he chose not to, he had to live with it, not her.

She lifted her chin in the air, determined to stay working. Her son meant the world to her. She had to let Duke know that it didn't matter that he didn't tell her everything. What employer did? After all, it was his business. Her son's future was at stake.

When she closed the gate, she saw him sitting on the porch at the table where they'd eaten supper last night. "Good morning, sir," she directed at him.

"Good morning, Miss Winslow. Can we talk?" he asked, standing when she got to the porch.

She didn't especially want to upset the apple cart as her mother would say, so she sat in the chair he offered.

"I want to apologize to you for simply not telling you the truth."

"I've come to the conclusion that as my employer you don't have to tell me anything about your personal life, sir. I'm here to work and earn extra money for my son's education. What you do or say is none of my business. Besides, if truth be told, you never said you had a wife or children. I assumed it to be so, even when it wasn't. So, you see, you didn't have anything to apologize for. My reaction was totally uncalled for." There, that should do it, she thought, satisfied all the right words came out.

He leaned in, causing her to look at him. When she did so, she saw the sadness in his eyes. It was quite disturbing. He looked very sorry. "I want to apologize to you as a friend, not an employer."

She was mesmerized by the look in his eyes. Did he value friendship the same as she did? If so, it was indeed a nice feeling. "Thank you. I'm not sure what to say, sir."

"It's Duke. Say it. As your friend, I give you permission to use my name."

"Duke." She knew it was silly to repeat what he said at will, but she was transfixed in his gaze. There was no way she was able to turn away. Those blue eyes of his were like magic and she wanted to be swallowed up in them. Oh, dear, this was madness. She just wanted a way to earn extra money.

"I would like us to be friends and I sincerely mean it, Martha. Do you mind if I call you Martha?"

"Not at all. I would like to be friends, also." The way he said her name gave her a reason to sigh deeply. He was so handsome and so kind to her, she was melting right here in his presence. He made it quite clear that his desire was to be friends. That's all.

Martha had convinced herself she never wanted another relationship again. She had believed it to be true. Yet, when she was in his presence, those words in her head seemed to disappear and all she wanted was to feel his mouth on hers. Oh dear, was she a trollop?

"I'm glad. I think we have a good start to a wonderful friendship, Martha. Shall we get started for the day? I thought I'd take some boxes out to the burn pile for you since I don't have any pressing business today."

Martha got up, hoping there was nothing in the kitchen that would point to her relationship with the former owner. Thomas Rider had been a slob. Most of the photos were most likely in the bedrooms or parlor. Maybe stacked in a box somewhere. But she doubted they'd find anything in the kitchen. Even so, she had to make sure. "If you'd like, I can cook some eggs for breakfast. I actually brought a few along from the doctor's back yard."

"The doctor's yard? How does he have time for chickens?"

She laughed. "He doesn't, but some of the patients don't have enough money to pay him so they give him a chicken as payment. He accepts it heartily. If you'd like some chickens for yourself, I'm sure he'd sell you a few at a great price."

Duke also laughed. "I don't know one thing about those birds. I've probably lived in the city for too long."

Martha laughed out loud. It was nice getting to know him. "I'm sure New York City has chickens somewhere."

Duke held the screen door open for her. "In the shops, already beheaded and feathered. I'll be in shortly, I've hired a young man to help weed the front yard. I see him coming down the street."

While Duke was outside with Tommy, one of the Martin boys, Martha quickly looked through some of the items laying about in the kitchen. There was no sign of any photographs that she noticed. A surge of relief went through her whole body. Maybe she'd have time to dig through some of the other boxes as well.

She cooked eggs for Duke and Tommy since she had already eaten this morning with her son, and poured them each a glass of milk. After setting the table on the front porch, she excused herself and went back inside, determined to get started. Before long, she had a huge pile of items that were going to the burn pile. Martha set everything by the back door to wait for Duke to help her lug it outside.

Between the three of them, they took three large piles of rubbish and old clothes out back. Duke found a tin containing matches on a shelf in the pantry and started a small fire. They all stood watching as the flames shot in the air about six feet high. Martha had brought out a bucket of water in case of flying sparks. "I don't want the grass to catch on fire. We'll ignite the whole neighborhood," she announced.

"You've done a great job with the kitchen so far," Duke said out of the blue. They stood side by side, the sparks staying contained. The ones in the fire and the ones between the two. Martha had to smile at the thought.

"Thank you. I will have the kitchen spotless by the end of the week and then on to the parlor."

"The parlor may take longer. There's so much stuff in there. Are you certain no one in town would want any of the things there?"

"No. Thomas Rider was sent to an asylum. I'm not sure if you heard the whole story, but no one in this town will take a thing from the mansion. They probably already think you are crazy to have bought it."

Duke chuckled. "I guess the place is supposed to come with a stigma. I can honestly say it isn't haunted if that is what people are worried about. My mother will love this old place."

"What about your sister? How old is she?"

Duke was quiet for a moment. "My sister is Tommy's age. She can't walk."

Martha stared into the flames for a moment. She stood alongside Duke, not knowing what to say. Why would someone buy this old mansion that needed so much work to bring a crippled woman here? Why uproot her like this?

"I'm sorry." She didn't know what else to say.

"She was in a riding accident a few years ago. The doctors said she'd never walk again. We've had her at some of the finest doctors to no avail. They all insist she would do better out in the mountains. We've been encouraged to come west to see if the change of atmosphere will help."

"Why would that make a difference? I don't understand." Martha thought maybe Doctor Frank could take a look at her and give him some advice.

Duke shrugged. "We've done all we can. Our so called step-father was making their lives miserable. When my mother found out he was selling her horses without her consent, she had him set up by a Pinkerton agent and he was sent to jail. My father's will explicitly mentioned that the owner of the horses were my mother and my sister and even if she re-married, they were not allowed to be claimed as marital property. The nightmare with my step-father caused my sister to become so depressed and ill, they thought several times she would not make it through the night."

"Is that when you began to look for a place here?"

"I saw an advertisement in the newspaper and bought this place, sight unseen. There really was no time to waste. My mother sold her farm to the neighbors and they are in the process of moving here. I am expecting them before the weather turns. I'd like to see them settled in by the first snow."

Martha laid a hand on his arm. "I will do my best to make sure this place is perfect for your family."

As the fire burned away the remnants of the past owner, Martha began to make plans to decorate the mansion for a family that was starting over. An idea was beginning to come to fruition and she couldn't wait until her shift at the doctor's office in the morning to talk it over with Mercy.

55

Chapter 8

Martha waved to Carson and hurried back to the doctor's office. Her son was getting to the point where any type of hug or kiss from her was embarrassing. After all, he was ten and didn't want to be kissed by his mother in public. It made her smile to know he was growing up and yet a twinge of regret that he was growing away from her surfaced.

She told Duke yesterday she'd finish her shift at noon and spend the afternoon washing down the walls in the kitchen. For now she was anxious to speak with Mercy, who was always supportive of her no matter what. Mercy had become a good friend this past year.

"You look quite happy this morning, Martha," Mercy quipped as she came through the front door. Going straight to the wash basin, she rolled up her sleeves and began to wash her hands the way Doctor Frank had instructed. He was always worried about contamination. It was something he learned about in medical school in Philadelphia.

"I am content, Mercy. There is something I want to discuss with you. Do we have time before the first patient?"

"Yes, our first patient is Mrs. McGregor and you know she is always ten minutes late. Come over here and sit down beside me. I want to know what you are all excited about."

Martha sat beside Mercy and explained what happened yesterday at Mr. Callahan's place. "So the fact is, he isn't a married man after all."

Mercy smiled. "And that makes you happy because there is certainly sparks flying everywhere between the two of you."

Martha shook her head. "That's not what I mean." Although it was true, she did realize they had feelings for each other, but she just couldn't afford a relationship with someone else yet. Not now. "Besides, I am recently divorced. It would not be proper to have a relationship with someone so soon."

Mercy flipped her hand in the air. "Piddly-do, Martha. Out here in the wilds of Wyoming, people are not as strict. As long as you treat others well and respect each other, all things are considered. Now, what did you really want to speak to me about?"

"I would like your help, and if you are willing to spread the word, I believe we can give the old mansion a beautiful transition. The town will never remember Thomas Rider ever lived there."

"I'm interested in hearing what you have to say."

"Mr. Callahan hired me to clean house and help him get rid of Thomas Rider's belongings. He is expecting his mother and sister in less than two months time. I'm afraid it will take longer than two months unless I have some volunteers who would be willing to help me transform the place into a wonderful oasis for a lovely lady who can no longer walk. The house needs so much. I can't possibly clean plus make the things that are needed for two ladies."

"What? His sister can't walk? That's terrible. I'm so sorry. Don't you worry, I'll help, along with others as well. I know some of the women with skills we may need. How about we have a meeting tonight after you get home?"

"I'd like that. Thank you for your help. I knew I could count on you, Mercy."

"We all help each other. Now, tell me about the mother and sister."

"They owned a horse farm in Kentucky and the sister got hurt in a riding incident. I'm starting to wonder if the evil step-father may have had something to do with that."

A sharp gasp came from Mercy when she explained what happened. "It wouldn't surprise me one bit. A man like that sounds so evil. Thank the good Lord he got caught and is in prison. May he rot in there until his death."

"I agree. What Duke's sister is going through must be horrible. She sits in a wheel chair and her mother is her keeper. But, his mother is not so young any longer. I may stay on as a housekeeper and caregiver if they decide to keep me. The problem is, I'm sure it is costly to bring them out here, especially with her special needs. I doubt they have much money now that the horse farm is sold, especially if that wicked man sold most of their horses. It's such a tragedy."

"That's very kind of you to want to help them by continuing to work as a housekeeper and caregiver. Perhaps you need to speak to him about it at some point," Mercy told her, placing a hand on her shoulder. "I wish you well and from the looks of things, it sounds like it may get serious between you and Duke. You did call him Duke instead of Mr. Callahan this last time, you know."

Martha's eyes widened in surprise at first and then they crinkled with delight. "I probably should not call him that in public, but he said we are friends and asked me to call him Duke. I also gave permission for him to call me Martha."

"Wow, things are moving along," Mercy told her with a lopsided grin. "I am happy for you, truly. You deserve to be happy."

Martha sighed. "I am happy. We have a roof over our heads thanks to you and the doctor and food in our belly. I've got two jobs now and am officially divorced from that man." She would never speak his name on her tongue again.

"Which is wonderful, but without love in your life, it can get lonely. That's all I'm saying. Don't ignore the feeling if it is right in front of you."

Martha stood when the doctor came through the front door. He was already out on his rounds this morning and ready to get started with the office patients.

"I think I see Mrs. McGregor coming down the sidewalk. I'll go meet her," Martha announced, ready to get away from Mercy's words. She agreed with her, but wasn't ready to hear it yet. Her heart was not ready to be broken in two and the fact was she had one broken heart from a man she had grown to hate. She wasn't ready for another one.

• • ❧ • •

MARTHA HURRIED UP THE path to the front door, thinking there was something different about the house already. Then she realized most of the front yard was free of tall weeds and the grass looked neat and tidy. It was actually much larger than what it had looked like now that all the ugliness was gone.

"It needs flowers next spring, don't you think?"

She was always pleased to hear his voice. She twirled around to find Duke standing in the yard with a pile of weeds in his arms. Tommy was raking the grass in the far corner, which is why she hadn't noticed him before. "Good afternoon. Yes, I think flowers in the spring would be lovely. You've got a much bigger yard than what I assumed."

"Tommy has been working hard all morning long."

"Great job, Tommy," she called out. "I'll be washing down the kitchen walls. In about an hour I'll take some of the lemons I brought with me and make fresh lemonade. How does that sound?"

Duke gave her a delicious smile. Wait. She didn't mean his smile was delicious. Well, maybe she did. Either way, he was smiling and it made her feel even lighter on her feet than ever.

"I'd love some lemonade," Tommy called out. He was working hard. She wanted to reward him even if she hadn't been the one to hire him.

"Will you allow me to pay you for the lemons?" Duke asked, his face serious.

"No, sir. You will not. The doctor has an abundance of lemons from one of his patients who brought them in from the train. He left the good doctor a bucket full. These were given to me to make sure you men quench your thirst."

"Please thank the doctor."

"You can thank him yourself," Martha called out. "He plans to stop by at the end of the day to check your stitches."

She heard him chuckle as she let the screen door slam behind her. This place, it felt almost like home. She loved the small house Mercy had rented to them, but knowing it was someone else's house was hard to really make it your own. This one, it felt different. She was clearing out the old and making it into a home for someone. Martha almost felt as if she were making it into her own home.

Except reality set in and she realized that wasn't going to happen. She would not allow herself to fall for a man again. No, sir. She was the housekeeper and a good one at that. And if she didn't' get busy, she'd lose this wonderful well paying job and she'd look out her window someday and see another woman in here doing her job.

Which very well may be a reality that she'd have to face in the future. A man like Duke would not stay single long in Belle. She could name a dozen women that would want to be his wife. The barn raising was coming up. Martha supposed he'd get a bunch of invitations from there. Instead of looking forward to the festivities, she almost dreaded it.

Well into an hour, she remembered to get the lemons squeezed and took a pitcher to the hard working men outside. "Come and get it!"

It didn't take long for Tommy and Duke to take a seat at the table. Martha almost wished she had some cakes for them to enjoy. She placed a hand on her hip and looked at them both. "Why, this won't do! Take those dirty hands and give them a cleaning before you sit at my table," she instructed.

Duke gave her a wink and followed Tommy to wash his hands at the outside pump along the side of the house. A few minutes later, they both had water dripping from their faces and hands.

"Much better. Here you go," she told Tommy, handing him a glass. When she gave a glass to Duke, their fingers brushed as a warm feeling rushed her from head to toes. This was nice. But, she wasn't interested in him in that sort of way. She had to remember that at all times. No matter what.

Besides, if he knew she was about to do some snooping around while they continued to work outside, he would not have a smile on his face like he did right now. Duke and Tommy were discussing the next project, painting the front porch. "I'll walk up to the mercantile and pick up the supplies we need."

"The front porch will look nice if it's painted," Martha chimed in. "I think if we ask Mercy, she may give up a few of her potted plants to make this look even more homey. Plus, now that I am here so much, it will be easier to take care of them."

Duke gave her a warm smile. "Thank you, Martha. My mother loves flowers."

It made her happy to offer them. She didn't think Mercy would mind at all. Making a mental note, she would wait until the porch was painted to bring them over.

"What are you drinking there?"

Martha waved. "Hello, Mr. Parson. Are you taking your daily stroll?"

"Yep, sure am. Then I saw what looks like lemonade. Now, I'm thirsty." He leaned against his cane a little harder, making it obvious he wanted to be invited, too.

"Come on up, Mr. Parson," Duke chimed in. "You don't need an invitation."

The old man grumbled something about it being polite to at least ask, but made his way to the porch like there was a fire lit under his feet. Martha looked to see Duke noticed too. He shook his head and shrugged.

Martha liked that quality in Duke. Helping your neighbor to feel welcome was important to her. Duke helped the old man sit at the table and refilled his empty glass, handing it to him. "I must get back inside since I only have a few more hours to work. Enjoy the lemonade, boys."

Once inside, Martha looked back to see the three men relaxing in the chairs and heavy into a conversation. She wanted to trudge upstairs to see if there was any chance of finding any revealing photographs.

There were three rooms upstairs. She went to the first room, finding a large bed and a dresser. The rest of the room was empty except for a carpet bag setting on the dresser. Was this where Duke slept? The floor boards creaked and groaned as she walked across them trying to be as quiet as possible. Even though they were outside, he may hear her up here. It was not where she wanted him to find her. Although, she could always say she was perusing the rooms for future cleaning.

Martha thought the floor would be so cold in the winter time. What it needed was a nice rug in front of the bed. How would his sister get upstairs to sleep? Would Duke have to carry her up? She tried to keep her mind on her task but found herself thinking of Duke the whole time she looked through the dresser drawers. There wasn't any evidence that Thomas Rider even used this room. After deciding there was no photos, she went on to the next room.

It was also empty. There was another smaller bed and one dresser against the wall. A small night stand sat beside the bed. Martha kneeled down and peeked under the bed. Nothing. She looked through each drawer to find no evidence there either. With a heavy sigh, she left the room and when she flung open the door to the third room, her heart fell to her feet.

Piles of clothing, a few trunks and frames with family photographs filled one wall. Martha hurried to the wall to search for the tell-tale photograph. There were so many. Thomas's mother had liked to spend money on card portraits throughout the years. She remembered her mother complaining how extravagant it was to have so many photographs.

Yet, her mother was one of the first to be there when the photographer was hired. Martha remembered having to pose several times as the whole family stood still until the man called out to them to freeze. She shook her head at the memory. Her mother was long gone, but the memory lived on.

Her eyes swept the room for any evidence of her younger years. Bright red color whipped in front of her from a photo on the wall. It was the one she had been searching for. The photo she had remembered being in. There was her family staring at the camera. Her mother, God rest her soul. Her father stood beside mama, making her smile. His long moustache always twitched when he laughed. He was long gone, too.

Memories rushed back and she never heard someone come up the steps. Duke's voice caught her off guard and she jumped in the air when he called out. "Martha, do you need help with anything?"

Her heart was racing so fast she thought it may leap right out of her chest and out the window to fall to its death in the front yard. She hurried to the stairs where he stood. "I was looking to see how much work these rooms will need. I know we are nowhere near starting them, but I wanted to get an idea. Follow me, I have a great plan if you'd like to hear about it."

Martha made her way past him and started down the steps, hoping he'd follow behind. She didn't want him to see the photo she had discovered. Even though it was hanging on the wall, she didn't think a stranger would notice a ten year old lanky girl. But her looks hadn't changed much.

She had to get rid of that photo, one way or another. Now that she knew exactly where it was, she'd find a way to make it disappear.

Before anyone else would ever lay eyes on it again.

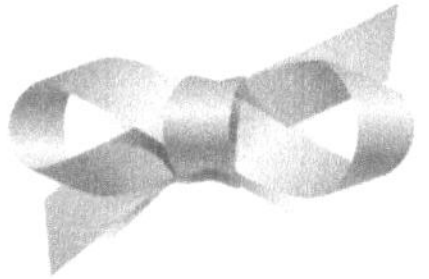

Chapter 9

"Didn't you say you had an idea?" Duke stood in the center of the parlor staring at her.

She almost forgot what she had told him upstairs, she was trying so hard to get out of that room before he discovered her secret. By the time they made it down the stairs, she had made small nervous talk about how the kitchen was coming along. She had kept her distance since every time he was so close it made her pulse quicken. "Did you know there are more rooms on the first floor?"

"I assumed there were, but hadn't checked. It's been quite busy since I've been trying to get so much outside work done because I know my mother and sister will love sitting on the huge porch."

Martha told herself he wouldn't think anything of her being upstairs snooping since she had discovered the extra rooms. He probably thought she was being curious since she had to do all the cleaning. Soon, the photo would be gone and she wouldn't have to explain to anyone again. She motioned for him to follow her. "This may look like an ordinary wall, but take a look at these fixtures. All we need is to find a way to open this up."

She had found the hinges the other day and realized Thomas had closed off the rest of the house since he'd been here. He had painted the wall and door the same, covering the hole where the door knob was so it appeared like it was part of the wall. She didn't know why he did it, but it was time to open up the large space she knew they'd find behind the door.

"I imagine there are more bedrooms or large open spaces. If your sister is in a wheel chair, this will be perfect for her bedroom so she won't have to be carried up the stairs. It will give her more freedom to get around the house."

Duke gave her an incredulous look. "That's nice of you to think of her." He felt around the perimeter of the door to see if he was able to open it by himself. But the paint had seeped into the frame around the door, sealing it closed. "I may need some tools to get this to open."

He went outside on the porch to confer with Tommy, who was arguing with old man Parson. When the two saw Martha and Duke come through the door, they both stopped and stared. "What is it?" Tommy asked.

"There is a door in the wall that probably leads to more space. For some reason it is sealed off and we can't open it. Tommy, can you run to the tool shed out back and find me something to pry it open?"

Old man Parson stood. "Follow me, young 'uns. You can just go through the side door."

"Side door? I never noticed any other doors except the front and back door."

"That's because the side door is covered with unruly bushes that I have to look at every single day. It's a disaster!"

Martha took Duke by the arm and pulled him along. "Come on, let's follow Mr. Parson. This is so exciting!"

The four of them trampled through the rubbish along the side of the house to discover the old man was right. Huge bushes covered a small side porch. A large French style double door opened easily when Duke turned the knob. "I had no idea," he said, stepping inside.

The old man stood a bit taller knowing he had solved a problem. Martha helped him inside and stood there, in awe of the huge room that had been hidden from the rest of the house. "This is lovely. All it needs is a little sprucing up. The perfect space for your sister, Duke."

"I believe you are right," he told her.

Martha walked around the room then, admiring the beautiful furniture still in the room. an Italian walnut bedroom suite sat in the room with a huge dresser on one side, a dressing table and matching bed posts and headboard. The intricately carved wood was not cheap.

"How in the world was Thomas Rider able to afford this type of furniture?" Martha knew his mother had inherited some things from a relative but she had no idea of the luxurious items in their possession.

"Your sister will love it," she said, running a delicate hand over the pattern.

Duke stood beside her. "I believe you love it as well."

She grinned. "It is quite exquisite. Any woman would be happy to have such a wonderful bedroom. I believe your family will love this old home."

He agreed. "Let's see the rest of this hidden wonder." She followed him through another door, to find a small hallway with three more rooms.

"This place is like a castle," old man Parson mentioned. "Why would that crazy idiot close this off?"

"Because he was crazy?" Martha shot out. The old man laughed and then shook his head.

"I believe the hallway is large enough Molly's wheelchair will not be a problem."

Martha agreed. "Let's take a look at the other rooms."

They followed each other into each room, discovering another room almost as big as the first one. Except it didn't have the open doors, but it did have a door to the large room. "This will be perfect for my mother. She can stay near Molly."

The next room was smaller, but again it had a door that led to the other. "This will make a nice sitting room for mother. That way she can have her privacy if she wants it."

When they went into the last room across the hall, Martha froze in the doorway. More photos filled the walls. One of them showed her entire family when she was about eight years old. As she studied the photos, she found another one where she was holding a fishing rod, along with several cousins and Thomas Rider in the background.

A fear so strong came over her, she closed the door. "There are some things in there that belong to the previous owner. I'll remove them as quickly as I can. Why don't we see if we can open the door to the parlor through this side. I see a door at the end of the hallway."

Everyone turned to where she pointed. Duke gave her a passing look and then followed the rest. She let out a huge sigh. Her heart was hammering like a woodpecker banging on a tree. She kept a few steps behind the rest to give herself time to calm down.

Old man Parson exclaimed in a loud, shrill voice. "Look, there's a key!"

Duke took a hold of the large pewter key and turned it. The latch sprung open with a click. He looked directly at Martha and grinned. Then he pushed his shoulder against the door several times until it flung open with a loud crack. The light that shot in lightened the whole hallway.

They were back in the parlor. "Tommy, that door comes off and stays off. I want this area open so my sister can manoeuvre her wheel chair through. Can you work on that this afternoon instead of working outside?"

"Yes, sir. I'll go get some more tools."

"I best be going home and resting. That was a lot of work we just did." The old man went through the screen door and headed home.

Duke and Martha shared a grin. "He must be utterly exhausted watching everything."

Martha giggled.

Duke smiled, his eyes crinkling at the corners. She lowered her eyes to the floor not wanting him to see how much she enjoyed his company. "I better get back to work," she told him, scurrying off to the kitchen. A bead of moisture dripped from her brow as she filled a bucket of water and soap to scrub the kitchen walls. This wouldn't take long but she had been interrupted twice today so she worked extra hard to get it finished.

Worry ate at her for the next few hours. She had to get back to that third room and collect all the photos. One way or another it had to be done. At three o'clock, Martha finished up, then went to find Duke. He was working side by side with Tommy, who was enlarging the opening to the hallway door.

When Duke noticed her standing there he looked up from the floor and smiled. "What do you think, Martha? Tommy made the doorway bigger so Molly's wheelchair can get through without getting stuck."

"That's a wonderful idea. Carson will be off school in a few minutes, so I must be going. I'll see you bright and early tomorrow."

She left before he was able to say another word. Worry that he'd go back in that room and take a closer look nagged at her the whole way to the school house. The sooner she destroyed the photo, the better she'd feel.

At this point, there was no way she could explain herself without lying through her teeth!

Chapter 10

Martha clapped her hands together. She had hurried to the mansion after dropping off Carson. He was going fishing again with the Martins after school, so she had a few extra hours to work. That would be plenty of time to get done what she intended to do today. "If I may have your attention, I'd like to organize a fire-burning day today."

Duke looked up from his plate of flapjacks. His cheeks were filled and all he could do was nod.

"Very well, then, I think it will be better if we empty out all of the prior owner's belongings instead of doing it room by room. This will get rid of everything at once and we won't have to worry about going back and forth. What do you think?"

Knowing Duke was filling his belly with her delicious recipe of thick, fluffy flapjacks, she wasn't giving him any time to disagree. She had her mind set when she arrived this morning. Her mother told her the way to a man's stomach was with food. Unfortunately, her prior husband had been mostly drunk and never took the time to sit and have a good meal.

It seemed to work with this group of men. Even old man Parson was coming over for breakfast every morning she cooked. He claimed to be out taking a walk, just like the doc had ordered. Then he'd give her that starry-eyed look and if she didn't invite him to eat, he'd grumble how no one paid any attention to an old man like him. She shook her head. The old man was lonely and finding a soft spot in her heart for him was not hard to do. Even if he did blurt out whatever came to mind first before thinking.

For the next few hours, Martha got busy, piling all of Thomas Rider's belongings from the parlor onto a pile she had started on the back porch. It had to be lugged from there to the burn pile, which was along the side of the house facing Mr. Parson's home. Once she made a pile pretty high, one of the two men would help to carry it the rest of the way to the burn pit.

Everything was going well. Old man Parson went back home to relax, his belly full. Tommy and Duke worked outside in the front yard while she worked inside.

Martha hurried down the hall to the third room they had checked the day before. More light was coming through the corridor now that the opening was larger. Light from the parlor shone down the hallway.

She turned the knob and went inside. Working quickly, she took the photo off the wall and slipped it inside her pocket. It left a large open spot on the wall anyone who walked in would notice.

Martha, began to take all the photos from the wall to make a pile on the night stand. Sweat poured down the side of her hairline, causing her to push strands of red hair back from her face. She'd feel much better when the photo was burned up and gone to ashes.

A pair of boots was heard coming down the hall, the sound of shuffling getting louder. Martha tried not to act nervous, but bent over a pile of household items and began to stack them alongside the photos. The one in her pocket was hidden from view except the corner kept digging into her thigh.

"You are quite the busy lady," Duke told her. "Here, let me get those for you." He took a pile of things from her hand and began to walk back out. "I was getting ready to start the fire when I realized we are out of matches. Tommy and I are going to walk to the mercantile to stock up on some things and pick up more matches. Is there anything you need?"

He sounded normal. Not suspicious at all. Whew! Martha grabbed a pile of photos on the stand and followed him out.

"Nothing I can think of. We should get this burned before the day is out."

"If not, we can have a bonfire tonight and watch everything go up in smoke like fireworks. Would you like that? You can bring Carson along."

"That may be nice, but we should get this burned as soon as possible."

"Don't worry, Martha. We have plenty of time."

I don't have lots of time! Instead, she gave him a smile as he got Tommy and they headed down Tall Pine Lane. Martha kept an eye on the two until they turned the corner. The moment they did, she hurried around the side of the house and stood in front of the fire pit. Everything was piled waist high. Duke and Tommy had packed everything together so when they lit it up, the fire would stay contained in one area.

Martha worked for another thirty minutes lugging the rest of the pile of personal belongings to the fire pit. Only then when it was almost as tall as she, her hand slid the photo from her pocket. Her heart began to pound so loud she looked around to make sure no one would hear it but her. The field that led to the sheriff's office and the main street was empty. Mr. Parson's house was the next house over, but he had said he was going to rest. She pictured him in his rocking chair, his eyes closed as he napped in the middle of the afternoon.

She held the photo in her hand one last time. "Finally, I got you. This is one photo that will never reveal anything about my old life again." She prayed to the Lord for forgiveness for having to stoop to this level to hide a family remnant, but it was for her son. He meant the world to her.

I'm sorry, Lord. I don't want to deny who my family is or its history, but people are so cruel. If they knew Carson was related to Thomas Rider, no one would allow their children to play with him. He'd be scorned and pushed away. Just like his father did to him, only it would be worse. Please don't let other people's sins affect my son's life.

She raised her head, held out the photo and shoved it halfway into the pile, buried deep in the center where no one would find it. Her hands shook as she finished the task. Soon, it would be ashes. Satisfied, Martha turned to go back inside and saw a shadow whizz past the window of Parson's kitchen. She froze. Had he been watching her?

When she tried to look closer, the shadow was gone.

Now, where did it go and what did that old man see?

• • ⚘ • •

"TOMMY, GO AHEAD AND help Martha finish lugging things out to the fire pit. I'll take this ointment over to old man Parson."

The doc had stopped him on his way home, apologizing for not following up as promised and reminding Duke he still needed to see his stitches. Doc Frank had an emergency so he hadn't been able to come over, which suited Duke fine. He didn't have time to dally at a doctor appointment, but the stitches did need to come out soon before they grew into his skin.

Duke promised the doctor he'd stop in first thing in the morning before he began working on the house. Besides, it gave him the opportunity to see Martha without the covering on her beautiful hair. She worked for the doctor two days a week and tomorrow happened to be one of them. He wished she'd take her covering off when she was working in his house, but every day it was tight around her head, covering those beautiful locks.

Some day he hoped to remind her that she didn't have to hide them. Sooner or later, she'd come out of her shell. He'd make sure of it. Duke knocked on the old man's door. "Mr. Parson?"

"Inside! Can't a man take a darn nap without being disturbed?" Duke opened the screen door and followed the grumbling. The old man was sitting in his rocker, his feet up on a large wooden box. His shoes were off and he had a cover over his mid section.

"Are you cold?" Duke asked, concerned. It was summer time, no reason to be chilled.

"I ain't warm, now, am I? Not with a blanket covering me!"

He seemed slightly agitated. Duke sat down on the settee close by. "I brought you more ointment from Doc Frank. He said to make sure you put it on right this time or he'll have to come check on you twice a day."

The old man waved a hand through the air. "That young doc is good at what he does, but if he thinks he is going to charge me twice a day for coming here, he's loco!"

Duke laughed. "He told me you'd say that."

"It's the darn truth!"

Duke figured he can't be feeling too bad otherwise he'd keep his trap shut more. "He told me to tell you he hasn't charged you a dime since you been going there. The doc said everybody likes you so much, he got donations from the townsfolk for your visits for the next five years!"

"Five years! Does he think I'll keel over by then?" The man actually looked affronted.

Duke did everything he could not to burst out in laughter. Somehow he knew that would upset the old man. There was definitely something wrong.

"What's bothering your soul, Mr. Parson?" Duke sat forward, determined to get it out of him.

Parson thought for a moment and shook his head. "I want to tell you something that you must promise never to repeat. Cross your heart and hope to die!"

Dukes stared at him. He wasn't going to promise something like that when he didn't even know what it was about.

Parson stared right back. "Go on, raise your right hand and say it!"

"I don't know if I should. I mean, how can you make me promise something that I don't know what it's about?"

The old man pulled the cover closer. "Either you do or you won't be able to help the one you've had your eye on now since you came to Belle."

"Martha? What do you know about her?" He was so confused now. Was the man going insane in his old age?

Parson put his right hand in the air and nodded to Duke.

He sighed. Then, his hand slowly went in the air. This was ridiculous. "Okay, I swear!"

"I swear to never let this secret leave this room."

Duke rolled his eyes. "I swear to never let this secret ever leave this room."

"You can roll your eyes, but if you say a word about this, it will ruin a young man's life. And a pretty young woman you can't take your eyes off."

Parson was either demented or worried. "I promise I won't ever say a word." After realizing his hand was still in the air, he dropped it. "Now, what's the secret?"

"The only reason I know this is because I've lived in this house since the Rider's first moved in. Mr. and Mrs. Rider were decent folk, but the boy, he was a strange one. Always going off by himself snooping in windows. He didn't start acting that way until he was about twelve."

Duke had work to do. He didn't want to upset Parson, but he had a pile of rubbish to burn and a yard to get done. "What does this have to do with Martha?"

"I'm getting to that," he grumbled. "You young folk can't be patient for more than five minutes."

"I've got work to do while the sun's up, sir."

Parson nodded in understanding. "Well, then I'll get right down to it. Turns out Martha is related to the family that lived in your house. Thomas Rider was her uncle."

Duke didn't see the problem. "She's never mentioned it during the time she's worked for me."

Parson shook his head vehemently. "No, no, no. She will never disclose that she knows. Can you imagine if the others in town found out? Why, poor Carson, whose been through enough grief in his young years, will be made fun of. The other kids won't let him live down that he has a crazy relative. I've seen it before. People don't try to be mean, but they are. If anyone knows what I know, it will destroy a beautiful woman and her son. Do you see what I am saying?"

"Why are you telling me?"

Parson pushed the blanket down from his lap. He leaned forward even more and pointed a finger at Duke. "Now, I'm not the brightest in the smart department, but I do know one thing when I see it and that's adoration for someone else. And I know a decent man when I see one. You are going to make that woman your bride and that boy your true son and give them a good life. That much I know for a fact!"

"I hadn't thought that far ahead, to be honest. I've got my own troubles getting my mother and sister here."

Parson shook his head. "That's where you are wrong, son. With the information I just gave you, it is now your duty to protect Martha and Carson for the rest of their lives. Do you know what she was doing today?"

He shook his head. Whatever Parson said next was not going to be a surprise. His head was spinning and he was having mixed emotions at the old man's words. He didn't see that it was a big deal having a crazy relative, but Duke guessed it was different here in Belle. "As far as I know, she was clearing the rubbish out of the house."

Parson nodded. "That's right. She was doing what you hired her for. Plus, she was searching and found something that obviously revealed she knew Thomas Rider. I saw her standing by the fire pile, then shoved a photo card deep into the stack."

Duke didn't think he could see that far. "Well, maybe she was just placing it there to get burned. It is her job to do so."

"Not when you look all around to make sure no one is watching you. She peered around both sides of the house and then quickly stuffed it in the middle. Why didn't she put it on top of the pile?"

"Maybe she was worried the photo would fly off?"

The old man waved his hand. "There's no breeze today, Duke. Now, you know I'm right. I know the exact photo she was trying to hide and I'll bet if I dug through that pile I'd find it right where she placed the dang thing."

Duke contemplated his words. "She's trying to protect her son. It makes sense. I'd do the same thing." For the longest time, he didn't want to take his sister away on excursions. He didn't want others to feel sorry for her or think she belonged in an asylum because she wasn't able to walk. For some reason, society as a whole thought if a person wasn't one hundred percent healthy, they weren't considered a productive citizen.

"She is trying to do all she can to protect him."

"How do you know so much, Parson?"

"I just do. Guess I'm her guardian angel. I didn't want her to ever find out that I know the things I do. Most of the others that knew are long gone. I'm the only fool left that remembers how she'd come visit with her parents and play with the rest of the kids. That bright red hair shined for all the world to see. Darn shame she has to hide her history, but she does. I promised my Lord I'd never tell a soul, except now I've broke my promise only to make sure she's going to be protected from her past. You're not going to let me down, are you?"

Duke wondered if the old man thought he was dying that he had to pass on the torch of this secret. He was getting quite used to Parson's morning visits.

This was a big deal to the old man and Duke wanted to reassure him that he'd never reveal what he now knew. His hand shot in the air. "I promise never to reveal what was just said inside these walls to anyone, ever. On my honor." He held out his hand to the old man, who shook it vigorously.

"Good. Now I can go to my maker without worrying about those two."

Duke was curious. "Parson, you aren't one bit sick and you certainly aren't going to your maker yet. Not as onery as you are! Are you trying to play matchmaker?"

The look on Parson's wrinkled face told Duke everything he needed to know.

Chapter 11

"Did you have fun at the Martin house?" Martha walked alongside her now growing son and listened as he told her about the fish he caught. She wanted to take his hand but he had let her know often enough he was too big to be holding his mother's hand or getting a hug or kiss in front of others.

"I caught a fish and it was huge, Mom. We cooked it for supper and Mr. Martin let me cut off his head."

Martha laughed. "Well, congratulations. That's a lot of work to get a fish ready to cook."

The boy shook his head. "You don't know the half of it, Mom. You can't just cook a fish. There is a lot of other stuff that goes on before you fry it up." He shook his head as if Martha could never understand the art of fish frying.

"I'm proud of you, son. How would you like to go over to Mr. Callahans? We are going to light the fire pit and afterwards have a treat on his front porch. Would you like that?"

Carson jumped up and down, his arms flinging from side to side. "Yes! I love fires! Can I light it? Please?"

Martha laughed. "I will ask Mr. Callahan. He may allow you to do so in front of him." She didn't tell him he was too young to light a fire on his own. He was touchy when it came to things like that. She didn't blame him. There were some kids who had already called him a mama's boy. Ever since, he'd been trying to act so grown up. Except at times she missed his snuggles and kisses.

"Are we going now?" Carson was still jumping as he walked.

She tousled his hair. "Yes, son. We must stop by the house to pick up the pie. I baked it last evening if you remember. It's been cooling since then, waiting for some hungry bellies."

He rubbed his stomach. "My belly is waiting on the pie, Mom."

"It will be awhile. Do you think your belly can stand it if we start the fire first?"

Carson nodded so hard Martha had to laugh. They hurried to the house to pick up the dessert and headed back to the mansion. They walked past the doctor's office, now closed. Martha almost dreaded having to work in the morning. It wasn't that she didn't like the job, but getting the mansion ready for his family was pushing her to want to finish what they started. Any interruption was just that, an interruption.

"Here we are. Why don't you go around the back to where Mr. Callahan and Tommy are working? I'll get the pie ready."

It didn't take much coercing to get Carson to go to the men. She busied herself in the kitchen, taking down four plates and forks, along with a large knife to cut each person a slice. On second thought, she reached up to grab a fifth plate.

She'd expect old man Parson to be on his way at any moment. If he was watching from his favorite spot at the kitchen window, he'd already know she had carried something into the house. One thing about living in Belle, the neighbor always knew what was going on. And yet, Mr. Parson had saved Mercy by being his nosey old self, which had prevented a tragedy. She'd be forever grateful to him so if all it took was feeding him then he deserved it.

"We're ready to start the fire," a voice came out of nowhere.

Martha jumped into the air, the pile of plates almost flying out of her hand. She caught them in the nick of time and turned to Duke. "I didn't hear you come in," she told him, holding the plates closer to her chest. She convinced herself it would keep her heart from pounding too loud.

"I'm so sorry. I didn't mean to startle you, Martha," he told her in a low tone.

She gave him a sad smile. "I'm sorry. Sometimes this house gives me bad thoughts. I have to clear my mind of them. Hopefully, when the renovations are done, there won't be any more reminders of Thomas Rider here. I've grown so close to Mercy and it saddens me that she may have been more seriously hurt the day he tried to kidnap her."

"Amen! I've heard enough about that man to make my head swell. Do we have all his things on the burn pile, Martha? I'm ready to get rid of it all, as you must be."

Goosebumps prickled her arms. Was he suspicious of her? Why did he say it like that, like she had a personal interest in this whole thing? She gave him a hard look. He seemed normal, like any other day. His eyes didn't pierce hers in an accusing way. It was her. She was nervous about the photo. She handed the pile of plates over to him and gave him a big smile. "As promised, I brought pie. Will you set these dishes out on the front porch table and I'll follow with the pie?"

Duke took the plates and headed for the front door. "Yes, ma'am," he teased. "The sooner we get the fire started, the sooner we can have dessert!"

This was going to be a wonderful evening, Martha thought as she followed Duke out the door. They both went out back where Carson was standing with Tommy, still jumping up and down. When he saw Martha, he ran to her and took her hand. "Can I start the fire, Mom? Duke said to ask you first."

Martha glanced at Duke. He was watching her son with amusement. "I don't see why not. As long as you follow the instructions to keep everyone safe. You know fire isn't anything to mess around with."

Her boy rolled his eyes first before running to Duke. "Did you hear her, she said yes!"

He jumped up and down in front of Duke, who swooped the boy up in his arms. "Now, listen here, young man. I'm going to let you start the fire, but I want you to follow my directions, okay?"

Carson nodded. The two talked awhile and Carson did as he was told. Soon, a roaring fire began to engulf the photos and belongings of Thomas Rider and his past. Martha's past, also. With the burning of the photo that sat in the middle of the pile, no one would ever be able to hurt her son. The past was now in a rubble of ash.

Carson and Tommy stood back from the fire while Duke stood beside Martha. She felt Duke's hand on her sleeve. When she turned to him, there was a fire in his eyes. He gazed at her, daring her to look away. She didn't. Perhaps this was the start of something new. Now that the jaded history was in the past, she'd be able to start over with someone. Someone like Duke.

It was probably just a dream though. Men weren't kind and loving. At least none that she ever knew. Her husband was a horrible man. At first he courted her and was cordial. But, the moment they married, all courtesy was gone and she became a slave to him. It was not a pretty memory. If only she could throw those past feelings in the fire and let them burn up never to remind her again.

Except they were scars that didn't just burn away. She imagined she'd have them forever. At least until someone came along and made her forget them. Was it possible Duke was that man?

He leaned in as the flames began to die down. "Martha," he whispered her name in a low tone. When she turned to look up at him, he leaned in further and placed a soft kiss on her mouth.

It was shocking at first and made her step back. But, then she surprised them both and leaned in, laying a hand on his shoulder and deepening the kiss. She felt Duke's other arm wrap around her waist.

Martha heard a giggle from behind her. Shocked at herself for behaving badly in front of her son, she backed away, placing fingers over her mouth. Her eyes widened in surprise. "I'm so sorry," she told Duke, then turned and took her son's hand. "Let's go eat some dessert!" she announced, pulling the boy along even though he insisted he was able to walk fine on his own.

When they turned the corner, old man Parson was sitting at the table, eyeing the pie. "Good evening, Mr. Parson."

"Martha, good to see you. I see you brought my favorite boy."

Carson shouted and ran to the old man, whose arms were outstretched for a hug, had no issue giving one to an old man. "It must be only mothers he won't hug," Martha mentioned, her mood already changing.

Duke laughed. "He's a good kid, Martha. He needs a father."

She turned to stare at him. "I can decide what is good for him."

"I didn't mean anything. I remember being that age. My father was a huge part of my life. Everything he did, I copied. Then when he died, there was no one. It wasn't fun growing up without a dad. After I left home, my mother was lonely and married a man who tried to ruin her. At least she was smart enough to get away from him. Like you were, Martha."

With those words, how could she stay angry with him. Martha blushed and followed her son to the porch, giving old man Parson a big hug. Anything to keep away from Duke. His presence was starting to disturb her.

How was she supposed to stay hard-hearted with a man around like him? She didn't want to love anyone. Not now, not ever. Well, maybe someday. Maybe, even Duke. The thoughts starting to fill her head were not good. She didn't want to feel this way. Not yet. So, what was she waiting on, she wondered?

"I love pie! How about you young man? Do you love pie, too?" Old man Parson took his fork and began to pound it on the table. Carson sat beside him in the chair, doing the same thing.

Martha scolded them both and looked at Duke who sat down with them. Before his fingers went for the fork, she shook her own at him. "Don't you dare," she mouthed, trying hard not to laugh. Taking the knife, she cut a slice for each hungry male, then one for herself.

The evening wore on, with laughter and stories from Parson's childhood. He had quite the tales to tell. Before she even realized, the night had crept up on them. Stars were scattered over the black sky, and a moon three-quarters full lit up the street. "We must be going, son," she directed to Carson.

He scooted back in his chair, holding out his hand to his mother. She was surprised and took it before he changed his mind.

"Go on," Duke told her. "We'll clean up."

"We will?" Old man Parson's voice sounded surprised.

"Yes, old man. It won't hurt you any to help now and again. You eat enough pie around here!"

Martha waved as she took her son home, who was starting to wear out. Tonight was a night she'd never forget. Looking back, she noticed Duke stood on the porch,watching them until they got to her house. She gave one last look back and waved before they went inside.

It had been a wonderful night.

The photograph was gone.

Forever.

Carson was free to live his life here without anyone knowing what a monster his uncle had been. She'd never have to worry again.

Relief washed over her. It gave her a renewed hope for a good future. Maybe she'd even consider another kiss from Duke.

Maybe.

Chapter 12

Martha, feeling groggy and yet happier than she'd been in a long time, hurried Carson to school. He was late waking up, too. They both had slept so good last night. She doubted anything would've been able to wake them up.

"I had fun at Duke's, Mom. Can we go again tonight?"

Martha was pleasantly surprised. "We'll see. We have to be invited first."

He shrugged. "I don't see why. Duke said I was welcome there anytime."

Martha nodded. "Yes, son. But, most people don't just show up, they ask politely to visit first."

Carson stopped. "That's not true. Mr. Parson shows up whenever he damn well feels like it. That's what Tommy said!"

"Tommy said that?" Martha made a mental note to speak to him about his language in front of her son.

"He sure did. Duke told him to mind his manners, but I heard Tommy grumble under his breath that he can say whatever he wants cause he is an adult now."

"Is that a fact? Well, Carson, even adults have to watch their tongue."

"Like this?" The boy stuck out his tongue, took two fingers and pulled it out in front of him. It made Martha laugh so hard, she thought she'd fall over in the street.

"Go on now, your teacher is waiting for you."

Carson waved to his teacher, turned and gave his mother a hug. "Thanks for taking me to Duke's house. I had so much fun I can't wait to tell the other kids. Wait until they hear I got to start a fire on my own!"

Tears sprang to Martha's eyes. It was the first time in a long, long time the boy was delighted and happy. All she had wanted as a mother was to give him a good life. The dark past had lingered on him more than she realized.

Was it time to give Carson a more secure home? One where a man was always there.

She hurried to the doctor's office, wondering what to do. Maybe Mercy would know.

After all, she was more knowledgeable in these matters since she was a married woman. Even though she didn't have any children, she had to have some answers. At least Martha hoped so.

"Good morning, Martha. You look quite flushed today. What have you been thinking about?"

Mercy had a cup of tea waiting for her. She waved Martha to the settee where they always chatted before the first patient arrived. Martha sat down beside her friend. "I'm so confused."

Mercy smiled. "I'm sure you are with that handsome Duke Callahan giving you those eyes."

"He gave me a kiss, too. Right in front of my son. It wasn't proper and I've been feeling quite giddy about the whole thing."

"Oh, Martha, this is so wonderful. A kiss! Now, that is progress."

She shook her head. "No, it's terrible! I'm not supposed to fall for someone the moment I get a divorce. How will it look to the town of Belle?"

Mercy shook her head. "Honestly, who cares! This town is filled with people with a past history that we know nothing about. It's best to keep those things tucked away in a closet somewhere."

She didn't tell Mercy about being related to the Rider family. She hated lying to her best friend, but it wasn't exactly a lie. It was more like an omission. She never wanted anyone to know.

The only other person who knew was that deadbeat ex-husband of hers, Ralph Winslow, and she hoped he'd never return again. He really had no reason to come back here. She had nothing to give him any more. He drank away their savings. She no longer lived in the same house so he wouldn't be able to find her. Besides, the sheriff would run him out of town before he got two steps inside of Belle. It was a comfort to know she'd never have to deal with him again.

As the morning wore on and patients were seen, she was pleasantly surprised when Duke came through the door. "Good morning, Martha. Mercy," he nodded to them both as he removed his hat.

"Come in, Mr. Callahan." Martha ushered him to a chair and began to take off the bandage. "Doc wants to take a look at your stitches and possibly remove them today."

"I had a nice evening last night," he said softly.

She stilled, not wanting to discuss her private life in the middle of a doctor's office. She felt his warm breath near her hair as she bent over his hand. He was teasing her. Why all of a sudden?

"Mr. Callahan, you finally made it. Let's take a look."

The doctor looked over the hand and decided to remove the stitches while Martha assisted. Each time she got closer to Duke, he would lean forward and nuzzle her hair. What in the world? He wasn't supposed to do that! If he were anyone else, she'd have called them out and the doc would've reprimanded him.

But, she didn't want to get Duke in trouble. His warm breath near her meant only one thing. He was a rascal and was deliberately trying to entice her. Maybe she should pinch him hard so he yells out and embarrasses himself. It made her giggle.

"Is something funny?" Doctor Frank asked. His hands, steady and sure, stopped in mid-air.

"I'm sorry, Doctor. I was thinking about my son and something he said last night," she lied.

She heard Duke chuckle.

"Let's finish up here."

Doctor Frank was serious when it came to his work. He took the last stitch out, instructing Duke how to keep the incision clean and instructed Martha to wrap up his hand. "Leave the bandage on for one more week. Even though it is healed and the stitches are out, you can never be too sure of getting an infection. Especially with you working at the old mansion. At least keep it covered for one more week."

Sometimes the doc was too cautious. Martha knew how Duke wanted to use his hand to help Tommy with the outside work. It looked like he'd have to suffer for another week. "Don't worry, Doctor Frank, I'll make sure he follows your orders."

"Very good. Thank you, Martha."

When the doctor moved on to the next patient, Duke whispered in her ear as she wound a bandage around his arm. "I'll see you in two hours. I have something for you."

When he left, her cheeks were bright red.

"Your blush matches the color of your hair," Mercy told her. "What's going on?"

"He told me before he left he has something for me." Her eyes were huge. "What do you think it is?"

"An engagement ring? An offer of marriage? I don't honestly know, Martha."

"It's too soon for all of that. I'm sure it's something to help me get my work done at the mansion. We've got to finish up in time for when his family arrives."

"You will get it done, Martha. Don't worry, and if you need to take time away from here to do so, you have my permission."

"I enjoy our mornings together. It's the only time I get to talk to another female."

"I feel the same way, Martha. I hope even after you are married you come see me. I know your life is about to change and no one deserves it more than you."

Martha gave her friend a hug. "That would be a nice thing to say if it were true, but my life is content. I'm happy to have a home and a job. Well, two jobs. Now I can send Carson to medical school without worry someday."

Doctor Frank walked in and must've heard the last part of their conversation. "You have that young man come see me soon. I want to show him what a doctor does. I can take him along on my rounds on Saturday morning if he'd like to go."

Martha was so lucky to have such wonderful people for neighbors and friends. "I'll ask him, but I'm almost certain he will be in heaven knowing he can go along. Thank you both. Now I must get to the mansion to work."

"Don't overdo it, Martha. If you need time off, let us know. We care about your good health."

"I'm fine, Doctor Frank. If I get fatigued, I'll let you know."

She left the office in a wonderful mood. The two of them always worried about her and it made her feel like she was a part of someone's lives. It felt good to have people who cared. She was taking a step in the right direction.

Martha made her way to her house, stopping off for a moment to pick up a donation one of the ladies sent over. She gathered it in her arms, ready to turn and go out the door when she heard a bump coming from upstairs. "What was that?"

She listened again but didn't hear anything. Martha wondered if Carson had placed his baseball on the dresser again. One time it had scared the daylights out of them when it rolled off the surface in the middle of the night. They were both a bit touchy about sudden noises.

Martha shook her head and pulled the screen door open. She took off towards the mansion, determined that every single noise was not going to get to her. Not anymore. Fear of her then husband storming in the house in the middle of the night drunk and mean were days that best be forgotten.

She had a new life to look forward to and she was walking right towards it.

Chapter 13

Duke had never been so nervous in his life. The table was set and he was now waiting for Martha to get here. He had told Tommy to stay away and do not interrupt them. He even sent him to old man Parson with a sandwich from the café so they'd be out of the way today.

When he spotted Martha coming down the street, he checked himself in the mirror on the wall in the parlor. His hair was combed and he dressed appropriately to pop the question.

He was going to do it today. Right now as a matter of fact. Why not? There was no time to waste. Martha had gotten her divorce and there was no reason for her not to say yes. He had promised old man Parson to protect her from her secret past.

By becoming her husband, he felt it was a sure fire way to protect her. No one would question her, even if they found out. Carson would have a father, a real father. He'd make sure of it. What could go wrong?

When Martha came up the steps and stood on the porch, Duke came out the door in his good suit. He took off his hat and set it on the small table beside the screen door. "Welcome, Martha. I brought lunch from the café. Soup and some fresh baked bread." He pointed to the small table they spent many meals sitting at. It was now dressed with a flowered tablecloth and two bowls filled with soup. The aroma of freshly baked bread filled the air.

Martha frowned. "Where is Tommy and Mr. Parson and why are you all dressed up? Are you going somewhere?" The confusion on her face made him smile.

He took her arm gently and guided her to the table. Pulling the chair out, he ordered her to sit. "Please, have a seat, Martha. We have something important to discuss."

"What is it? Is everything alright? Have I done something wrong?" A real fear was taking hold of her and Duke knew it probably had to do with the photo she had wanted burned. Was she still worried about that revealing photo card? Well, she didn't have to worry any longer.

"Let's eat first. I'm sure you must be starving."

"I am hungry." After they said grace, they dug into their food and ate silently. Martha still seemed confused, but he acted as if this wasn't anything extraordinary.

"Good, eat up. I've got something special for dessert."

Twenty minutes later and with little talking, their plates were empty. Duke was hardly able to hang on. He wanted to get this over with. The anticipation was killing him. What if she refused? Doubts were starting to overwhelm him.

"That was delicious, Duke. What do you have in there for dessert?" She was starting to relax now, which did make him feel a little better. Still, his nerves were shot.

He stood, leaned over the table and picked up the silver plate with a lid on it he borrowed from the café. "I'll give you the pleasure of opening it."

"Is it cake or pie?" She rubbed her hands together and reached for the lid.

His heart almost stopped. What would she do? He stared at her lovely slim fingers as they took hold of the handle and lifted the lid.

A small box sat in the center of the plate.

"What is this?" she whispered.

Duke picked up the box and slid to one knee. She stared at him, her eyes huge.

He opened the lid. "Martha, I know we haven't known each other long, but in my heart I know you are the one I want to spend the rest of my life with. Life is too short to wait any longer. Will you marry me?" His words were simple. He'd explain more later.

"Marry you?" she whispered, the words barely tumbling from her sweet lips. "I don't know what to say. Duke, you can't possibly want to marry me!"

The fear in her eyes was real. He laid a hand on her arm. "Yes. I do want to marry you. Truly, I do."

Her face didn't change. "This is such a shock."

It wasn't going well. She was supposed to be happy and jump for joy. Wasn't she? "I know. I've thought about it for the past three days, Martha. We work so well together. Your son needs a father."

She frowned. "Is this about Carson? Do you want to marry me to give Carson a father?"

"I want to marry you because it's the right thing to do."

"I'm your housekeeper, Duke!"

"I want that to change to my wife."

"I'm utterly in shock."

"I still want to marry you."

She shook her head and stood. "It's too soon. You scare me, Duke."

He frowned and stood facing her. He laid both hands on her shoulders. "I scare you?"

"Not you personally. The thought of marrying again scares me so much. That horrible man was sweet until the day I married him. Then he became a monster. I can't do that again. No matter how much I want to be held by you. No matter how much I want you to kiss me every single day. No matter how much I don't believe you are like him, I'm scared, Duke. I am so scared."

She let a tear fall. Duke gazed into her tear-stained face, not knowing what to say. He grew angry at the horrible man who instilled this fear in her. Maybe it was too soon. "I'm sorry if I asked you too soon, Martha. Please, don't cry."

That brought on more tears. He pulled her into his arms and held her there until she pushed away, her beautiful eyes staring back at him. "I truly care for you. I do. Can we take it slower, please? I know you want to be settled when your family comes, but I can't move any faster. I pray these terrifying feelings go away soon."

He nodded, then closed the box. "This ring will stay in my pocket until you are ready. You'll see, Martha. I'm not going anywhere. I'll be right here when you are ready."

Her shoulders relaxed under his hands. She let out a deep sigh. "Thank you, Duke. I'm so sorry."

"No need to be. We must get to work. My family will be here in a matter of weeks."

She lowered her eyes as if shy all of a sudden. He placed a hand under her chin. "Do me a favor, Martha. Hold your head up high. You don't need that covering on. Wear your hair like you do in the doctor's office. It's beautiful, like you are." He placed a kiss on the tip of her nose and left the porch, heading to the back of the yard. He needed some time alone.

Duke picked up an ax by the wood pile and began to chop a large piece of wood. His bandaged hand held the handle, causing him to wince after awhile. He switched hands and pounded into the wood, taking out his frustrations on the wood until Tommy came along and pulled it from his hand.

"You're going to annihilate that poor piece of wood, Duke. What's wrong?"

Duke stood back, his chest heaving. "She said no."

Tommy shook his head. "Parson said she'd say no. He said it was too early."

"How does that old man think he knows everything? Did you tell him about my plans?" Tommy had been the only person in town he'd talked to about the proposal. Frustration was building up again. Duke had planned for this proposal for the last twenty four hours, even asking the jeweler to open shop early to choose a ring.

"He knows because he was in town early this morning and saw you knocking on the shop window before they were opened up. Told me the minute I got to his house with lunch today. I didn't have to say a word to him. Besides, I wouldn't spill the beans when you asked me not to."

"I appreciate that, Tommy. Let's get to work."

"I think you should know, Martha left to pick up her son. She said she was going to come in Saturday morning instead and work then. She hurried down the street like a rattlesnake was chasing her."

Duke knew the boy didn't need picked up for another two hours. He hadn't wanted to chase her away. That was not the plan. He grabbed the ax from Tommy's hand, pounding into the wood again like nobody's business.

Tommy stood and watched him, staying clear out of his way this time. Duke needed the hard work, to vent his frustrations and chide himself for being such a fool.

Chapter 14

Martha had spent the majority of the afternoon sitting on a bench down by the creek. She hadn't told anyone where she was. Listening to the water run across the rocks was soothing and gave her time to think.

She had been too hard on Duke. The feelings she held were hers alone. Why was she so afraid to marry again? It had been a long time since her husband had gone away. By now, the two of them were settled and happy.

But she had been lonely. It was hard to live alone without arms to hold her each night. She had longed for her husband to do so for many years but he was too busy getting drunk.

Being in Duke's arms made her realize that she did need him. She wanted to be married to him and wake up each day with a smile on her face. Life was too short. Duke was right.

Leaving the peaceful area, she hurried to the school to find Carson wanted to spend the night at the Martins. They promised to take him along fishing Saturday morning. After she agreed to let him stay, she walked past the shops in town, contemplating what to do next.

Martha turned around quickly when she felt someone watching her. She stopped in front of the café and looked in the window. A few townsfolk waved to her and she smiled and waved back. Nothing unusual there.

The feelings going through her were strange. It felt like the nights she wasn't sure if her husband was coming home in a good mood or bad one. The fear she was allowing to creep in startled her. Martha had to get over this. It was not normal to feel so mixed up.

She needed to speak with Duke. Making up her mind, determined to finally make her stance, she marched down Tall Pine Lane and knocked on his door.

The mansion door opened slightly. When Duke saw it was her, he opened it wider and stepped onto the porch. Tommy had gone for the day and old man Parson was settled in his chair. At least he was supposed to be. She stared at Duke, who looked worried.

"Can we talk?" she asked, raising her chin a notch.

"Please, let's sit." He led her to a bench on the other side of the porch. Sitting beside her, he turned to listen.

"Duke, I was wrong."

She felt him take her hand gently in his own. The warmth overwhelmed her. She almost began to cry, but kept it together until she said what she came here to say.

"I love you."

That threw her off. "What?"

"I have been chopping wood all afternoon long. I worried myself to death thinking maybe I asked you to marry me too soon. But, Martha, what is too soon? Can't two people who get along like we do begin to love without having to have a time line? I mean, why can't we love each other so soon?"

She smiled. "There is no timeline when it comes to love, I'm afraid."

"You feel it too, then. Do you love me, too, Martha?"

"I'm afraid I do, Duke." She took his face in her hands and looked up at him. "It's why I came back. To tell you that I want to marry you."

He pulled her to him, gently pressing his mouth to hers. They kissed for the longest time, a gentle yet loving kiss that sealed their fate. When he pulled away, he leaned his forehead against hers. "I want to have the biggest wedding this town has ever seen."

"Oh, Duke. I don't need a big wedding."

He shook his head. "My mother will be here. She will want to help you. My sister will help you, even though she can't walk. She is quite crafty in other areas. You deserve the biggest wedding of your life."

"It would be fun to plan. But, first, promise me we will get this place in order. If there is any money left over, then we will plan a big wedding."

He agreed with a condition. "Only if I can have another one of those kisses."

She giggled and pressed her mouth to his.

A sigh followed, with a whole lot of kissing.

• • ⁂ • •

MARTHA WATCHED DUKE as he walked back to his house. They spent the evening talking, then he walked her home. She gave him another kiss at the door and sent him away. "I'll see you first thing in the morning. We can spend the whole day getting the parlor finished. I think after that, we can finish the bedrooms and decorate the porch."

"Everything is going as planned," Duke told her. "I got a telegram from Mother today telling me they'll be leaving in two weeks time. Which means they may get here earlier than planned."

Duke had explained before it would take them longer to travel since his sister needed extra care. He had hired a caregiver for her during the trip. His sister did a lot of her own care, but she needed help to get on and off the trains. His mother did a lot, but she was getting older now and deserved to rest.

After he turned and waved, Martha made her way inside. She locked the door and lit the oil lamp, its glow lighting up the parlor. It was always so quiet when Carson wasn't home, even though that wasn't too often.

Stretching, she took the oil lamp up the stairs and prepared for bed. Another thump against the floorboard caught her by surprise. More curious than anything, she went into her son's room. She held the lamp up, aiming it towards the dresser. His baseball was there, sitting on a piece of cloth so it wouldn't roll off.

Martha listened again.

Another thump.

It sounded as if it were coming from his bed. She turned to her son's bed and held the lamp over the mattress.

Martha gasped!

Her worst nightmare was right here in her son's bed!

He turned, his arm flailing against the wall, causing the bumping noise she heard earlier.

"Ralph Winslow, what are you doing in my son's bed?"

His eyes fluttered open. They were red and glassy. He was inebriated. Again.

A small fear tucked itself into her chest, but she pushed it away, determined not to be afraid. She took a few steps towards the door, realizing if she ran he'd come after her.

Unless he was so drunk he wasn't able to walk. But, that never happened. He seemed to have super human strength when he was drinking.

He sat up. "Where are you going, wife?" he accused, rubbing at his eyes. His feet were planted on the floor and if she didn't answer he'd spring up and come after her.

Martha needed a weapon. She took a slow step backwards. "Why are you here?"

"I'm here to see my wife and son."

"Your son is spending the night somewhere else."

"Where!" his voice roared.

Martha almost shrunk back from his shouting but then she held her feet firm on the wooden planks and stared him down. She didn't have to protect Carson since he wasn't here. She'd stand up to this man and face him once and for all. She was tired of being a victim to his mean nature. "It's not any of your business. After what you did to him, the sheriff will run you out of town. I suggest you leave before you get caught."

He stood, towering over her and yet she wasn't quite as scared as before. "I'm not going anywhere until you clear out that bank account and hand me over the money. I need to get away before the snow keeps me here for the winter."

"I have no money." She wasn't going to give him a dime. She worked for everything she had. All he ever did was take.

"Not according to that sweet little lady leaving the doctor's office earlier. I asked her if she knows you and she said you usually work for the doctor, plus you work for some man who now owns the mansion. What's going on with that, Martha! Why are you kissing a strange man? You are my wife."

"I'm no longer your wife, Ralph. We've been divorced for some time."

He looked furious. "Why haven't I been notified?"

"How? You left here with a woman on your arm for the whole of Belle to see, making a mockery of our marriage. No, you don't deserve a dime of the money I worked hard for. Get out!"

He strolled over to her, lifting her chin in the air, his putrid breath almost suffocating her. "I'll go when I say it's time to go. Where do you keep your money? Is it under your mattress?"

"No."

"Well, where is it?"

"I don't have any."

"I'll tear this house apart. I've already looked in every nook and cranny in the kitchen. If you don't cough up some money, I'll ruin everything you own."

Fear caught a hold of her even though she tried hard not to let him see it. If she didn't sound afraid, he usually calmed down. Well, most times he did. "I have twenty dollars saved. That's it."

"That won't get me to where I want to go."

"Where are you going? If it gets you out of my life, I'll give you the twenty dollars." She resigned herself to losing the money. If it was the only way to get him to leave, she didn't care. She could work longer and harder for more money.

"I'll take the money. What else do you have here worth a few bucks?"

"Most of the things here belong to the doctor's wife, Mercy. She owns the property."

"A doctor's wife? Maybe we should have the doctor and his wife come over. I'll bet they have some money."

"No! Do not involve anyone else."

"What about your boss? The one I hear you've been visiting every day? I bet he has some money."

"He will not give you any. Look, Ralph. Let me go downstairs to get the money and I won't tell a soul. You can take my wagon and horse." She'd tell him anything to get out the front door.

He was still half drunk, teetering as he tried to hover over her. The problem was, Martha had one thing in mind. She was no longer afraid. He had no one to hurt any more, or throw in her face. He'd always threaten her with hurting Carson and she'd give in to shut him up. Without Carson here to get hurt, she was able to face him a lot less fearful this time.

"Go on, go get the money, but no funny stuff." He reached in his pocket and pulled out a knife. Opening the blade, he held it in front of him. "I'll use it on you."

Martha hurried down the stairs, leaving the lamp in the room. In complete darkness, she felt her way to the front door, quickly turning the latch.

"You forgot the lamp. How are you going to find the money?" he said, stumbling towards the landing at the top of the stairs. "Hey, where are you going? Get back here!"

Martha flew threw the open door and began to run. She lifted her skirts and ran towards the mansion, calling out Duke's name. In the still of the night, she sounded like a wolf howling in the night.

She didn't look back, afraid Ralph would catch her. As long as she got onto the front porch, she knew old man Parson would notice the commotion. She was going to scream at the top of her lungs.

She was done fighting for her life. She needed help and knew exactly where to go.

Chapter 15

Duke's eyes shot open. His foggy brain was desperately trying to focus. He had been dreaming, but through the pleasantries, a voice was calling out to him. "Duke! Duke!"

He jumped out of bed, peeking out the window to see Martha, her skirts flying all around her, running up the street towards his house. He pulled on a pair of britches and ran downstairs in the dark. Flinging open the door, he rushed outside to feel her body fall into his open arms. "What's wrong? Martha? What is it?"

"It's Ralph! He was hiding in my house and he wants money."

Duke saw a shadow running towards the mansion. He pushed her through the door. "Lock it behind you. Do not come out no matter what."

Duke noticed a light shining in old man Parson's place. The screaming must've woke him up. He heard the screen door slam in the distance.

There was no longer a shadow but a man standing on his lawn. Tommy had oiled the gate so it no longer squeaked. "Who goes there?" Duke asked, full well knowing who it was.

"I need some money to get out of town. I asked her real nice to get me the twenty dollars she promised me. Instead, she flew out the door and ran here. She's still my wife I don't care what divorce papers say. I never got any. She owes me."

Duke had enough. The man was done threatening her. "You take yourself off my property before you get hurt."

Ralph laughed. "I ain't leaving until I get my twenty dollars."

"You gonna get a shot in the arse is what you gonna get!" Old man Parson was holding his six-shooter in both hands in front of him. He was wobbling on his feet, his hands shaking like crazy. Now Duke had to worry about him, too.

"Put that gun away, Parson. I'll handle this."

"No way. I hit my target even with these shaky hands, son. This man has caused enough damage. It's time he met the Lord."

"Ain't no one meeting the Lord on my watch. Hands in the air, Winslow. You are under arrest for several things. I have a list a mile long but murder is at the top."

Duke heard Martha open the door. "Murder?" she asked, stepping outside and standing beside Duke. He placed a protective arm around her. She was still shaking and breathing heavy.

The sheriff of Belle nodded. His pistol was pointing into Ralph Winslow's back, daring him to make the wrong move. "Yes, sir. He murdered Dolly Clanton, the saloon girl he rode out of town with. That's a hanging crime."

"He don't look so tough now, does he?" Martha mentioned.

Duke pulled her closer. "He sure don't. Go on, Sheriff Knight. Get him off my property."

Martha stepped forward. "Sheriff, did you know he was in town this whole time? I mean, where did you come from? I was running for my life a few minutes ago and you were nowhere to be found. The street was empty." She placed a hand on her hip. Duke was worried she'd fly off the handle.

Sheriff Knight tied the man's wrists together behind his back and took Ralph by the arm, still holding a gun over him. "I'm sorry folks. I knew he was here. Been waiting on him, but I had to catch him and he was hiding. I'll be taking him to jail." The sheriff looked at Martha. "You don't ever have to fear this man again. I'll be taking him to justice in a few days. He'll be hung for his crimes."

Martha let out a sigh of relief. "I don't condone hanging, but if he killed someone then he sure deserves it, doesn't he?"

The sheriff nodded. "He deserves what's coming to him. No one gets away with breaking the law in my town."

Martha, relieved and glad that Carson didn't have to see what just happened leaned closer to Duke. As she did so, Ralph glared at her.

"Did you tell your beau the horrible secret you've been hiding from the town? Did you?" A loud thump had everyone staring at the man who just slumped on the ground. The sheriff lightly mentioned how the prisoner's head accidentally hit the back end of his pistol. "That was an accident." He noticed his deputy coming towards him. "Deputy Will, help me get this man to jail."

Between the two of them, they lugged his body off, never to be seen on Twin Pine Lane again.

Martha was staring at Duke, the fear back in her beautiful eyes. Old man Parson had parked himself on the porch step, breathing heavily. His pistol lay alongside of him.

Duke turned back to her, wanting to take the fear from her eyes. "Martha, I know."

She hesitated, frowning. "What is it you know, Duke?"

He shrugged and took her hands. "I know about Thomas Rider. I know he is your uncle," he said, his words quiet and meant for her ears only.

She tried to turn away, but he held her hands in his. "No, Martha, don't run from me. What I know stays right here. Parson already told me and I'm still here. He's always known, but he never told a soul until I came along. For some strange reason, he thinks he's going to his grave and wanted to make sure you and Carson are taken care of."

"Truly? You know and you don't care?" Tears streamed down her cheeks.

He shook his head. "I don't care, darling. But, I understand you never want anyone to know for Carson's sake. He may want to know about his family someday."

She nodded, trying to wipe at her tears. Instead of letting her hands go, Duke lifted their hands together and with his fingers, began to wipe away the tears. He placed a kiss on her cheek.

"Maybe someday when he is a grown man I'll tell him, but now, he's been through too much. I need him to have a normal life."

"He will. I promise you that, Martha. On my honor." He placed a hand on her cheek and took her other hand and placed it over his heart. "Do you feel my heart beat?"

She nodded. "I do."

"It's all for you, darling. I want to marry you and make Carson my son. I love you. And there's something else I didn't tell you. I have enough money to take care of you and put Carson through medical school. You won't have to work two jobs anymore. I'm kind of rich."

She gave him a hug. "I love you, Duke."

"I love you both," Mr. Parson called out, a tear slipping from his scraggly old face.

Martha laughed and ran to him, sitting beside him and folding him in a huge embrace. "We love you, Mr. Parson."

Duke watched them laughing together. He was so happy right at that moment. He kneeled down and took her hand. "Will you take this ring now?"

He had forgotten to give it to her yesterday. She held out her hand while he slid it on her finger. "Perfect."

She stared at the ring, then looked up at him. "It is perfect, just like the man who wound up stealing my heart after all."

Thank you for reading Stealing My Heart. Would you like to read all of Cyndi's Belles of Wyoming in one shot? You can get her boxed set, available now! Save $$$ with a boxed copy. Get [1]Cyndi[2]'s Boxed Set - Belles of Wyoming Available on Amazon![3] (https://www.amazon.com/gp/product/B08XPS4W26/)

---

1. https://www.amazon.com/gp/product/B08XPS4W26/

2. https://www.amazon.com/gp/product/B08XPS4W26/

3. https://www.amazon.com/gp/product/B08XPS4W26/

Keep reading for other books by Cyndi Raye

Cyndi's other books

Mail Order Brides of Wichita Falls Series

Ruby

Grace

Lily

Charity

Hannah

Rebecca

Sophie

Ellie

Jenna

Leila

Boxed Set Vol 1-8

Christmas in Wichita Falls Holiday Book

Brides of Mill Ridge Series

An Outlaws Honor

A Reverend's Rose

The Ranger's Redemption

A Doctor's Devotion

A Teacher's Treasure

A Sister's Sanctuary

Sons of Nora White Series

A Bride for Luke

A Bride for Adam

A Bride for Samuel

A Groom for Nora

A Bride for Russell

A Bride for Wesley

A Groom for Widow Young

The Pistol Ridge Series
Peg Leg's Princess
Blaze's Beauty
Judge's Jewel
Rider's Renegade
Raven's Rebel
Preacher's Pearl
Creed's Confidant

Multi-Author Series Contributions

A Bride for Abel - The Proxy Brides Book #4
A Tin Star for Christmas - The Belles of Wyoming
Mercy's Gift - The Belles of Wyoming
Candy Cane Christmas - Ornamental Matchmaker Book #10
A Bride for Calvin - The Proxy Brides
An Agent for Caroline - The Pinkerton Matchmakers
An Agent for Cari - The Pinkerton Matchmakers
Stealing Her Heart - The Belles of Wyomng

CONTEMPORARY SMALL Town Romance

Florida Keys Romance in Paradise Series

The Tomorrow Serial
The Forever Serial
Escape Serial
Island Keeper
No Name Inn Series
Boot Key Harbor Short Story Boxed Set
Santa's Wrong Turn & Save Me Santa Holiday Shorts

All these books can be found by visiting https://www.amazon.com/Cyndi-Raye/e/B00ENA1WEG

Don't miss out!

Visit the website below and you can sign up to receive emails whenever Cyndi Raye publishes a new book. There's no charge and no obligation.

https://books2read.com/r/B-A-PXQ-SHTDC

BOOKS 2 READ

Connecting independent readers to independent writers.